William Davies

A Fine old English Gentleman

Exemplified in the Life and Character of Lord Collingwood

William Davies

A Fine old English Gentleman
Exemplified in the Life and Character of Lord Collingwood

ISBN/EAN: 9783337013523

Printed in Europe, USA, Canada, Australia, Japan

Cover: Foto ©Raphael Reischuk / pixelio.de

More available books at **www.hansebooks.com**

A

FINE OLD ENGLISH GENTLEMAN,

EXEMPLIFIED IN

THE LIFE AND CHARACTER

OF

LORD COLLINGWOOD.

A Biographical Study.

BY

WILLIAM DAVIES,

AUTHOR OF 'THE PILGRIMAGE OF THE TIBER,' ETC.

LONDON:
SAMPSON LOW, MARSTON, LOW, & SEARLE,
CROWN BUILDINGS, 188 FLEET STREET.
1875.

PREFACE.

AS this volume is not intended to form a complete biographical account of the events of the life of Lord Collingwood, but to be an analysis of his character based upon them—that is to say, the circumstances of his life being considered in their bearing on his character, and not with respect to their own importance—I have not thought it necessary to encumber my text with notes of reference, but have satisfied myself (and I hope I shall have satisfied my readers also) by giving an initial list of the various sources from which the material for my study has been for the most part derived. For this reason the reader must not look for a strictly consecutive or exhaustive account in these pages of Lord Collingwood's career. For these I must refer him to the authorities specified, which I have not in any way attempted to rival or supersede, but only to supplement by a review of what has been there presented to me. Those who would desire to pursue the subject further, or to obtain a fuller account of the circumstantial portion of Lord Collingwood's life and its political surroundings, will find in the authorities I have given ample means of doing so; especially in the valuable series of letters and memoir edited by Mr. Newnham Collingwood, to which my little essay is largely indebted.

LIST OF BOOKS PRINCIPALLY MADE USE OF IN
WRITING THIS VOLUME.

———

' A Selection from the Public and Private Correspondence of Vice-admiral Lord Collingwood: interspersed with Memoirs of his Life.' By G. L. Newnham Collingwood. Fifth edition, 2 volumes. Ridgway and Sons, 1837.

' Lord Collingwood's Register Books of Correspondence and Orders, &c., from 1782 to 1809.' 7 volumes. Manuscript in the British Museum.

Memoir of Lord Collingwood appended to Clarke and McArthur's ' Life of Nelson,' 1840.

James' ' Naval History of Great Britain,' 1859.

Brenton's ' Naval History of Great Britain,' 1837.

Ralfe's ' Naval Biography of Great Britain,' 1828.

' Despatches and Letters of Lord Nelson,' edited by Sir N. H. Nicolas.

' Naval Chronicle,' various volumes.

' Edinburgh Review,' Vol. 47.

' Quarterly Review,' Vol. 37.

Memoir of Sir H. Blackwood, Bart., in ' Blackwood's Magazine,' Vol. 34.

' European Magazine,' Vol. 57.

' Gentleman's Magazine,' Vol. 80.

Alison's ' History of Europe, from 1789 to 1815.'

Lord Dundonald's ' Autobiography of a Seaman,' 1861.

———

₊ The portrait prefixed is engraved by C. H. Jeens after a mezzotint by Charles Turner, from a painting in the possession of Lady Collingwood in 1811.

A few engraver's proofs, printed on large paper, suitable for the portfolio or for framing, may be had of the publishers, price 5s.

A FINE OLD ENGLISH GENTLEMAN.

IN an age when morality is regarded as a branch of speculative science, as a tilting-ground whereon polemical disputants may break lances, its practical aspect for the most part set aside or forgotten; when philosophy in its highest office and function, as an instrument of self-government, is ignored, and made instead the football and plaything of school-men; when churches are fighting for the figments of creed and dogma, hampered in ceremonial and ritual, mocking a high behaviour with functional observance, and hedging in the Christian sympathies, which ought to be as wide as the world, to the limitations of a pinched and lean ecclesiasticism, or, on the other hand, using religion as a mere emotional exercise; when men seek public offices for the purpose of promoting private ends, and make a good profession subserve an indifferent practice; when merchants and tradesmen strive

B

above every other thing to be rich, and even the
wealthy to add land to land and gold to gold
greedily, or else find their whole delight in the
pleasures which money can buy, and set aside all
others as of little worth; when the wholesome and
natural restrictions of conscience, not only with the
ignorant and professedly vicious, but with those who
claim to be numbered amongst the most respectable
of the community, have to be delegated to the
province of legislation; so that before we can believe
a statement of the genuineness of the simplest
article of commerce in quarters which ought to be
above all shade of suspicion, there must be a re-
assuring Act of Parliament upon it: amidst all this
it is refreshing to turn to the example of one to
whom right was the sole law, in whom self-interest
had no place, whose religion was centred and contained in the fulfilment of actual duty; to one, in
short, who, living in these later times, maintained
the splendid old rules of a noble life, and what is
more, lived up to them.

I do not mean to depreciate the age in which we
live. I am well aware that our social and civil
economy is in many respects better regulated now
than it was seventy or eighty years ago. Intelligence
has spread, charitable institutions flourish, society
has repaired and is repairing some of the most
crying evils which formerly existed. But are there

not others still prevalent amongst us, not less pernicious because they are not publicly scandalous? Do we not see office filled by incompetency and indifference, unscrupulousness in business, workmanship vamped up anyhow so that it be paid for, virtuous principle practically derided, and true heroism—the heroism which sacrifices itself to duty, entirely disregarded? Of course there are exceptions, very many and noble exceptions to all this; but are they not exceptions, and not the rule? It is strange that with all our churches, chapels, school-boards, and other moral and religious engines, we cannot so much as produce an honest, upright, and conscientious community in the mass. Does it not show that there is something fundamentally wrong or insufficient in our religious teaching and education which allows them to exist side by side with the most virulent and insidious social evils, which, as long as these evils are clothed with a conventional speciousness, permits them to be disregarded in our churches, in our schools, in our families, and in every relationship of life?

It is a very bad sign when a nation makes little of its heroes; when it can afford to set by the great deeds of great men as things of small importance, or to forget them in the pursuit of wealth, business, or pleasure; when its pulpits ring with declamatory platitudes, and the heroic life is left unexpounded, uncommented upon; when youth is pointed to the brave spirits of old, and those of his own age and race are unnoticed or sparely and rarely brought before him; when he is taught to regard the remote and shadowy characters and conceptions of antiquity as models of life and conduct, and is allowed to overlook in a greater or lesser degree the examples of his own time and country, however splendid. For, indeed, every good, true, and well-ordered life is an epic which outshines that of Homer, and transcends the narrative. The sublimest efforts of art reach nothing so grand as a noble and disinterested life, nor are they so touching and elevating. It is with pain that we must be brought to allow that there is no place for any systematic teaching of the practically heroic in the conduct of life in any instrument of modern education : that either the standard set before us in our churches and schools is an imperfect or false one, or else that the means used to enforce it are utterly inefficient and incompetent to do so.

But, although this is true generally, happily there are those still amongst us who, valuing profession and emotion at their real worth—that is, just so far as they bring their votaries to a large, virtuous, and noble life, and no farther—know how to reverence genuine magnanimity and self-devotion, and to treasure them in memory as sacred things. If ancient Greece and Rome had their heroes, England has had her heroes too, and, let us hope, has them still, not less great, if less famous. She can point to her warriors, her martyrs, her divines, her philosophers, and to brave men and women not included amongst these, though not less high-minded, who have fought the great battle of life against fearful odds and have conquered.

Of two kinds of greatness I know not which to place before the other: that which is unflinching in adversity, which holds its own against every opposition, which yields not so much as a hair's breadth of its high standard, however pressing the temptation of personal advantage, however much trouble may be saved by a dereliction of principle; or that which belongs to power unabused, the fine reticence which, endowed with a choice of action or administration, only adopts that which is right; which looks to no supervision for its rule of conduct, but bears within itself the character of an immutable justice, the principles of an unchanging truth, uncorrupted, disinterested, and absolute; which looks upon the gift of power as a stewardship, as a function held for the fulfilment of certain duties in which the officer is but the instrument of administration, and, without arrogance, insolence, or assumption, is content to be the servant of something better than self.

Doubtless these two qualifications are to a certain

degree interdependent and potentially coexistent. A consistent individuality would include both were circumstances to require their exercise. Of the latter in particular we have an example in recent times, than which there is no nobler in any other, in Cuthbert, the first and last Baron Collingwood.

Cuthbert Collingwood came of a good lineage— an ancient and distinguished family in Northumberland, whose name was loved and feared long before he was born. At the Raid of Reidswire, a border skirmish between the English and Scotch in 1575, in which the Scots were victorious, Sir Cuthbert Collingwood, one of his ancestors, was taken prisoner with the lord-warden and other nobles and knights, and is thus celebrated in a ballad reprinted in the 'Border Minstrelsy:'

> " But if ye wald a souldier search
>   Among them a' were ta'en that night,
> Was nane sac wordie to put in verse
>   As Collingwood, that courteous knight."

His great-grandfather carried arms for Charles I., and had his property confiscated on that account; and later still George Collingwood of Eslington suffered death for his attachment to the House of Stuart in the rebellion of 1715; his lands also being forfeited to the crown. He is thus addressed as a friend of Lord Derwentwater in a ballad called 'Derwentwater's Good Night.'

> " And fare thee well, George Collingwood,
>   Since fate has put us down ;
>   If thou and I have lost our lives,
>   King James has lost his crown."

The family having been thus reduced in circumstances, Lord Collingwood's father settled at Newcastle-on-Tyne, and marrying Milcah, daughter of Reginald Dobson, Esquire, of Barwess, had three sons and seven daughters. Of these Cuthbert, the eldest son, was born on the 26th of September, 1750. Of the character of his mother I know nothing. That she was the worthy parent of such a son I make no doubt ; as the highest kind of greatness is rarely attained without some part of it, at least, being attributable to a mother's early influence. Cuthbert was sent to school at Newcastle under the tutorship of the Rev. Hugh Moises, who lived to see his pupil grow to an eminence creditable to himself and to all who had had any part in his training and education. At the same school were educated the brothers subsequently Lord Stowell and the Earl of Eldon, the latter of whom used to speak of Collingwood in after-life as having been a " pretty and gentle boy." At the early age of eleven he was sent to sea, then a rising service, under the care of his cousin, Captain, afterwards Admiral, Brathwaite. To his careful training under this able and judicious commander he attributed much of his knowledge of seamanship

and the duties of the service. A touching circumstance meets us in our first acquaintance with his
personality. When he first went on board his ship,
his mother's tears still wet on his cheek, the poor
little fellow sat down and wept. No wonder that
his heart should sink within him at the utter un-
friendliness and unhomelikeness of everything around
him: I dare say it was the bitterest moment of
his life. As he thus sat, the first lieutenant,
seeing his forlorn condition, came to him, and with
words of consolation and encouragement strove to
raise his drooping spirits, which so touched the
heart of the boy that he took him to his cabin and
offered him a large piece of plum-cake which his
mother had packed into his box:—a very tender
incident, indicative of much that lay at the foundation of his future greatness, simplicity and nobility
of character. I should like to have shaken that
kindly-hearted lieutenant by the hand.

Collingwood's early life is marked by no important circumstance. Indeed, very little is known
about it, as he was far too modest to make either
himself or his concerns matter of notoriety. No
doubt, as he grew in stature he grew in wisdom also.
No doubt he learnt by stern experience, and, in the
varied incidents of a seaman's life at that time, came
to a pretty accurate knowledge of himself, and found
out of what sort of hard material the world is for the

most part made. A kind of autobiography which he was induced to give in after-life to a periodical publication of the day—the 'Naval Chronicle,' in which it occupies the modest proportion of just three pages—consists of little more than a series of dates, with scarcely any personal detail. He was not the man to use many words in talking about himself or his doings.

Of Collingwood's fifty years' service in the navy, about forty-four were passed in active service; from 1793 to 1810, he was only one year in England, and once he was twenty-two months at sea without dropping anchor; a circumstance almost unprecedented in the annals of sea-service at that time. He was nearly thirty before he got promoted above the rank of lieutenant. He says, by way of preface to the autobiographical notes above alluded to:—

"My life has indeed been a continued service at sea, but unmarked by any of those extraordinary events, or brilliant scenes, which hold men up to particular attention, and distinguish them from the number of officers who are zealous and anxious for the public good."

He remained with Captain Brathwaite many years. He afterwards went with Admiral Graves to Boston, on a supply expedition during the American War of Independence in 1775, and was there landed with a party of seamen to assist the troops at the battle of Bunker's Hill; upon which occasion he acquitted himself in so notable a manner that he was made a lieutenant, his commission dating from the day upon which the battle was fought. In 1776 he went to Jamaica in the *Hornet* sloop, and was soon after joined by Nelson, then a lieutenant in the *Lowestoffe*, with whom he had already formed a very warm friendship. Here was stationed Sir P. Parker, Commander-in-Chief, who, being friendly to both, in advancing Nelson, appointed Collingwood to take his place. It thus happened that Collingwood followed the steps of Nelson, first in the *Lowestoffe*, then in the *Badger*, of which Collingwood was appointed commander in 1779, and afterwards in the *Hinchinbroke*, a 28-gun frigate, which made them both post-captains. In 1780 a plan was formed for crossing the Isthmus of Panama by water; an ill-digested proposal in those early days of engineering which ended disastrously for the expedition. Nelson, stricken with fever, had been obliged to abandon the station; but although Collingwood suffered several attacks, he was enabled to resist them all. In four months one hundred and eighty out of the two hundred composing his ship's crew had died from the virulent nature of the climate. In the month of August Collingwood was relieved, and in the following December appointed to the command of a small frigate, the *Pelican*, of 24 guns. Eight months afterwards, in one of the cyclones which not infrequently devastate these regions, Collingwood's ship was thrown on the rocks of Morant Bay in the middle of a fearful night; the next day the ship's company managed to reach shore on rafts constructed from the ship, and afterwards spent ten days on a barren and sandy island, with little food, and undergoing severe privation. They were afterwards rescued from Jamaica. Collingwood next commanded the *Sampson*, of 64 guns, which was paid off at the peace of 1783; upon which he took the command of the *Mediator*, and went to the West Indies, where he remained until the latter end of the year 1786.

Here we have almost all the incidents of Collingwood's early life given by himself: but how much do they cover! What patience, what fortitude, foresight, and bravery are here implied! The long schooling to sea-ways and sea-life, the earnest study, the strong self-government necessary to save himself from a more disastrous shipwreck than it is within the power of the elements to cause—the moral shipwreck which destroys so many hundreds and thousands on the rocks and quicksands of life, flinging them from wave to wave, or sucking them down to gaping whirlpools remorselessly. Without the training of a father's care or a mother's gentler hand to draw out the best feelings of the heart, he had to maintain all the nobler faculties of his mind and nature by the power of his own will. He had to fight the battle of

life under peculiar disadvantages as regards its moral
conduct; how great those disadvantages were, may
be inferred from the circumstance that so few com-
bat them unscathed. Not that the maritime life has
not produced, and does not constantly produce, heroic
men and fine-spirited, adventurous characters; but
it very rarely develops these high qualities except at the expense of some other. It is rare
to find, as the results of such a training, the hard
qualities of endurance, bravery, nerve, and energy
united to the more sensitive gifts of great warmth
of heart, a love for domestic relationships and the
social life, with an acute tenderness which is pained
by the sufferings of the most insignificant creature.
It is seldom that we find temperance without
austerity, bravery without impetuousness, or temerity,
careful judgment and consideration without hesitancy,
the most uncompromising strictness in fulfilling and
enforcing duty without severity, the most scrupulous
honesty without littleness, the utmost care and
economy without meanness or illiberality, dignity
without pride, and honour without arrogance. It is
seldom that we see the most perfect knowledge and
punctuality united with patience towards stupidity,
and forbearance towards incapacity, carelessness, and
folly; the utmost gentleness with the greatest firmness; a mind capable of appreciating the finer
elements of the elegant arts combined with a power

to face storms, shipwreck, disease, and the cannon's
mouth without a tremor—yet all these qualities and
many more as good and as great were comprehended in
the character of Lord Collingwood. He knew how to
obey as well as how to command, to rule as well as to
serve. Such men make their world; it is not made
for them; they control the elements, overrule the
revolutions of time, and supersede the reversions of
circumstances. Lord of themselves, they hold the
whole world in subjection. For, indeed, this is a
victory worth all the rest: to conquer oneself; and
then every other conquest is easy.

Imagination may be permitted to linger a moment
over two circumstances in the above narrative.
First on that dreadful Mosquito shore of Central
America, with its attendant horrors. What a
terrible situation! A squadron over which Death
was the head commander! Day after day he
unrolled his black banner, floating it at each mast-
head. Day after day the hot sun rose and fell, and
added to the tale of victims. Many of the ships
were changed to vast coffins, with never a living
soul in them, and drifted and sank in the harbour,
weary of the day and their sore burden. One may
picture to oneself the brave captain of the *Hinchinbroke* as he walked the deck at the evening hour,
after the fiery heat of a tropical day, his ship
transformed to a hospital, and no remedy of any

avail to save his diminishing crew. How would his
heart be filled with sorrow, with sweet sad thoughts
of home and friends beyond the far seas, as Death laid
a fevered hand upon him also, shaking his dark
lance over his head, only forbearing to strike! To
meet a visible enemy had been easy, to contend
with a mortal foe a thing without terror; but this
invisible, insidious, and insatiable assailant, who
could look upon his inroads with indifference or
regard his approaches without a shudder? As the
commander saw the vessels—ghostly hearses of the
dead—around him in the harbour, with their tattered
sails and dismantled rigging, or their dropping
shrouds a dark network across the moon's disc, how
would his senses be oppressed and his soul choked
and suffocated under the irresistible dominion of the
arch-conqueror! It would be almost like a realiza-
tion of the terrors of the 'Ancient Mariner:'

> "I looked upon the rotting sea,
>   And drew my eyes away :
> I looked upon the rotting deck,
>   And there the dead men lay."

Yet the undaunted captain endured it all. No
doubt he would keep up his inspection of the sick;
no doubt he would order his ship as well as possible,
and be content to be doing his duty under circumstances of so much horror, in the midst of scenes so
appalling.

Another striking picture is presented to us in the shipwreck he suffered shortly afterwards, when stranded upon the rocks at midnight, the tempest raged around, and every moment threatened destruction. Though he fails to tell us so, we may be certain that his voice would be heard above the storm and the roaring of the sea, heartening the sailors to their task, and cheering them to struggle for dear life. Then we see them toiling over the surf on their frail raft till they reach the strand. But what a desolation! A long, flat, sandy shore, and nothing else but sand! Day after day with little to support life, they watch the tossing billows around them, night after night they lie down weary and unprotected, suffering almost every want, and hardly snatch a few hours of perturbed repose. At last help comes. The brave spirits have not wrought and expected in vain. They regain the mainland exhausted and half-starved; only the indomitable British courage and energy unquenched within them.

It may be mentioned that in the account of himself and his doings from which the foregoing sketch is taken, Collingwood omits to state that shortly before his shipwreck (of which he was exculpated from all blame) the *Pelican* (his ship) had captured *Le Cerf*, a French frigate of 16 guns, and recaptured the *Blandford*, a richly-laden vessel from Glasgow, under very creditable circumstances.

When Collingwood went to the West Indies in 1783 he took with him Captain Moutray and his wife, the former of whom had been appointed resident naval commissioner at Antigua. They afterwards became fast friends. Mrs. Moutray, writing to Mrs. Newnham Collingwood, Lord Collingwood's daughter, many years afterwards, gives an insight into his character which may not unfitly find a place here.

"Previously to that time," she says, alluding to the period of her residence abroad, " I had only known your father as an agreeable acquaintance: for perhaps I need not tell you that although the vigour of his mind was soon discovered, there was a degree of reserve in his manner which prevented the playfulness of his imagination and his powers of adding charms to private society from being duly appreciated. But the intimacy of a long passage in his ship gave us the good fortune to know him as he was, so that after our arrival at Antigua, whenever he was at St. John's or in English Harbour, he was as a beloved brother in our house."

When Mrs. Moutray returned to England in 1785, she made Lord Collingwood a present of "a trifle": a purse she had netted for him, for which Collingwood returned the following graceful verses of thanks:

> "Your net shall be my care, my dear,
>   For length of time to come,
> While I am faint and scorching here,
>   And you rejoice at home.

"To you belongs the wondrous art
To shed around your pleasure;
New worth to best of things impart,
And make of trifles—treasure."

Nelson being stationed at the West Indies at the same time with Collingwood, they frequently met at the commissioner's house, and a life-long friendship was cemented between them.

The station was occupied at this time for the purpose of preventing the trade of the United States, which had been proscribed by convention, with those possessions. Unfortunately the navigation laws were not so clearly laid down as to be beyond dispute. Nelson, after seizing several ships, was much harassed by arrests and law-suits, through which, however, he was supported by the English government. In a letter to Mr. Locker, written in 1784, when on this service, Nelson gives a hearty testimony to Collingwood's goodness and worth. He says, "Collingwood is at Grenada, which is a great loss to me; for there is nobody that I can make a confidant of." Again, he writes a little later, "Coll. desires me to say he will write you soon such a letter that you will think it a history of the West Indies. What an amiable, good man he is! All the rest are geese." Once more he writes from the *Boreas*, off Martinique, in 1786: "This station has not been over pleasant: had it not been for Collingwood, it would have been the most disagreeable I ever saw." Nor was this kindly feeling entertained on the one side only. It was fully reciprocated by Collingwood. "My regard for you, my dear Nelson," he writes in 1792, "my respect and veneration for your character, I hope will never lessen."

From the latter end of 1786 to 1790 Collingwood was at home in Northumberland, making acquaintance, as he says, with his family, to whom he was almost a stranger. Soon after his arrival at home he received a sympathetic letter of condolence from Nelson, informing him of the death of his brother Wilfred, who had been captain of the *Rattler*, also on the West Indian service; an active and promising young officer, whom Nelson deeply mourned as a friend. He says, "Collingwood, poor fellow, is no more. I have cried for him, and most sincerely do I condole with you on his loss. In him his Majesty has lost a faithful servant and the service a most excellent officer." During this visit to England in the year 1787 Collingwood wrote a letter to a young officer which ought to be charactered in letters of gold in every ship in the navy. It shows the principles by which he himself was guided and governed, and how early he had adopted them. It is full of sound philosophy and sterling common sense, and reflects as much credit on his head as on his heart. It is dated in London, Nov. 7, 1787.

"Dear Lane:—It gives me great pleasure to find by your letter that your situation is agreeable to you, and I hope it will always be so. You may depend on it, that it is more in your power than any one else's to promote both your comfort and advancement. A strict and unwearied attention to your duty, and a complaisant and respectful behaviour, not only to your superiors, but to everybody, will ensure you their regard; and the reward will surely come, and I hope soon, in the shape of preferment: but if it should not, I am sure you have too much good sense to let disappointment sour you. Guard carefully against letting discontent appear in you; it is sorrow to your friends, and triumph to your competitors, and cannot be productive of any good. Conduct yourself so as to deserve the best that can come to you; and the consciousness of your own proper behaviour will keep you in spirits, if it should not come. Let it be your ambition to be foremost on all duty. Do not be a nice observer of turns, but for ever present yourself ready for everything; and if your officers are not very inattentive men, they will not allow the others to impose more duty on you than they should: but I never knew one who was exact not to do more than his share of duty, who would not neglect that when he could do so without fear of punishment. I need not say more to you on the subject of sobriety, than to recommend to you the continuance of it as exactly as when you were with me. Every day affords you instances of the evils arising from drunkenness. Were a man as wise as Solomon and as brave as Achilles, he would still be unworthy of trust if he addicted himself to grog. He may make a drudge, but a respectable officer he can never be; for the doubt must always remain, that the capacity which God has given him will be abused by intemperance. Young men are generally introduced to this vice by the company they keep: but do you carefully guard against ever submitting yourself to be the companion of low, vulgar, and dissipated men; and hold it as a maxim, that you had better be alone than in mean company. Let your companions be such as yourself, or superior; for the worth of a man will always be ruled by that of his company. You do not find pigeons associate with hawks, or lambs with bears: and it is as unnatural for a good man to be the companion of blackguards. Read —let me charge you to read. Study books that treat of your profession, and of history. Study Faulkner's Dictionary, and borrow, if you can, books which describe the West Indies, and compare what you find there with your own observation. Thus employed, you will always be in good company. Nature has sown in man the seeds of knowledge; but they must be cultivated to produce fruit. Wisdom does not come by instinct, but will be found when diligently sought for; seek her; she will be a friend that will never fail you. You see I am writing to you as one very much interested for your welfare. Receive it as a proof that I shall always have pleasure in hearing of your success. Give my best respects to Captain Brown. I am infinitely obliged to him for the favour he did me in taking you; and I hope you are showing your gratitude to him by your best exertions. Remember, Lane, before you are five and twenty, you must establish a character that will serve you all your life. I hear Bennet, my dear boy Bennet, is with you at Jamaica; if he is, remember me kindly to him; cultivate his friendship, for he is a

sensible and an honourable young man. I wish you
good health : and be assured of the regard of, my dear
Lane, your sincere friend."

With such sentiments as these a man could not
fail to secure the foundations of a true and great
life, for such words are its soul and crown. Friend
to himself he would find the whole world friendly, or
make it so. Nothing could go very much amiss to
one anchored upon so true a basis. On him the whips
and scorns of time would fall comparatively lightly.
Blame or praise would not furnish the rule of life
to him who held a nobler standard far above them
both. He could afford to lift his head higher than
the world's estimate. Its rewards could not make
him rich, its detractions could not impoverish him.
The paltriness of time and place service were as far
removed from him as they are from honesty : the
contemptible intrigues of meanness and selfishness
find no place with such a code. To such souls the
world goes round in a smoother course. They can
never be bankrupt, for their wealth is a fountain of
perpetually flowing satisfactions. They look over
the horizon and see the land of rest lying calm and
still beyond the tossing of the seas, the roaring of
the tempest, the storm and the thunder, and are at
peace—peace with themselves and the whole world,
for their name is Peace.

Another voyage to the West Indies in the *Mer-*

maid in 1790, when the rupture with Spain was anticipated, and once more we find Collingwood at home, without any present prospect of further demands on his services.

At this time he was married to Miss Sarah Blackett, the daughter of John Erasmus Blackett, Esq., who was a younger brother of Sir Edward Blackett, Bart., of Newby Park, Yorkshire. This was in every respect a most happy marriage, and had only the drawback of Collingwood's subsequent long absence from home. Two daughters were the sole offspring; Sarah, born in 1792, and Mary Patience in 1793. "I now thought," he says, continuing his autobiography, "that I was settling myself in great comfort; but I was mistaken; for in eighteen months the French War broke out, and in 1793 I was appointed captain of the *Prince*, Rear-Admiral Bowyer's flagship, and served with him until he was wounded in the action of the 1st of June, 1794, in the *Barfleur*." Collingwood's account of this battle is full of interest, though, as usual, he fails to give an idea of the part which he took in it. With a stroke of affecting tenderness he says they first sighted the French fleet "on the morning of little Sarah's birthday," and after an account of the sharp but not decisive engagement of a previous day, thus describes the battle:

"On the 30th, we first saw them far to leeward, but it

was foggy and bad weather, so thick, that we could scarce see the length of the ship, until the 31st., in the afternoon, when it cleared, and we observed the enemy to leeward forming their line. We bore down to them, and formed ours, which took us all the evening. The night was spent in watching and preparation for the succeeding day; and many a blessing did I send forth to my Sarah, lest I should never bless her more. At dawn we made our approach on the enemy, then drew up, dressed our ranks, and it was about eight when the admiral made the signal for each ship to engage her opponent, and bring her to close action, and then down we went under a crowd of sail, and in a manner that would have animated the coldest heart, and struck terror into the most intrepid enemy. The ship we were to engage was two ahead of the French admiral, so that we had to go through his fire and that of two ships next him, and received all their broadsides two or three times before we fired a gun. It was then near ten o'clock. I observed to the admiral that about that time our wives were going to church, but that I thought the peal we should ring about the Frenchmen's ears would outdo their parish bells. Lord Howe began his fire some time before we did; and he is not in the habit of firing too soon. We got very near indeed, and then began such a fire as would have done you good to have heard. During the whole action the most exact order was preserved, and no accident happened but what was inevitable, and the consequence of the enemy's shot. In ten minutes the admiral was wounded; I caught him in my arms before he fell; the first lieutenant was slightly wounded by the same shot, and I thought I was in a fair way of being left on deck by myself; but the lieutenant got his head dressed, and came up again. Soon after, they called from the forecastle that the Frenchman was sinking; at which the men started up and gave three cheers. I saw the French ship dismasted, and on her broadside, but in an instant she was clouded with smoke, and I do not know whether she sunk or not. All the ships in our neighbourhood were dismasted, and are taken, except the French admiral, who was driven out of the line by Lord Howe, and saved himself by flight. At about twenty minutes past twelve, the fire slackened, the French fled, and left us seven of their fine ships—*Sans Pareil*, 84; *Juste*, 84; *L'Achille*, 74; *Northumberland*, 74; *L'Amérique*, 80; and *Le Vengeur*, 74, which last sunk the same evening; so that you see we have had as complete a victory as could be won."

He adds:

" Several lieutenants are killed and wounded, and this, altogether, has been the hardest action that has been fought in our time, or perhaps ever. It did not last very severely much more than two hours, when ten of the enemy's ships were dismasted, and two of ours. They were superior to us in ships, men, and guns, sent out for the express purpose of destroying us. Four of their ships were provided with furnaces for red-hot shot, one of which stuck in the *Royal Sovereign*, but I have not heard that they did any mischief in any part of the fleet by them. We understand their orders were to give no quarter, and, indeed, they fought as if they expected none."

It was in this engagement that the true heroic

element in Collingwood's character comes out, as noble in his fearlessness as he was unselfish in honours to be won. On the fall of the admiral the command of the ship devolved upon him. After he had crippled his antagonist, seeing the *Invincible* (English vessel), near, he resigned his half won, or, rather, virtually altogether won, victory to his friend, who was unfit to engage an uninjured ship, whilst he went forth to attack a fresh vessel. How careless must he have been of accredited honours and how true to his cause! By what a simplicity of purpose must he have been ruled! With what an elevated principle must he have been animated! How absolutely must he have been possessed with all that is comprehended by the term magnanimous!

And what was the reward of all this fine conduct from a grateful country? It was that it should be utterly and entirely ignored. It was that whilst other and inferior officers received insignia and distinction, Collingwood should not only have had none of them, but that his name should not even have been mentioned: so that whilst the English nation rejoiced on account of its great victory, the name of one of the chief instruments of that victory was passed over publicly in silence. Not so privately, however. "If Collingwood has not deserved a medal," said Pakenham, the gallant commander of the *Invincible*, "neither have I, for we were together the whole day." "I do not know a more brave capable, or a better officer in all respects than Captain Collingwood," said Sir George Bowyer, in a letter to Admiral Roddam. "I think him a very fine character; and I told Lord Chatham, when he was at Portsmouth, that if ever he had to look for a first captain to a commander-in-chief, I hoped he would remember that I pledged myself he would not find a better than our friend Collingwood."

Bowyer had learned and well knew his value. The whole fleet was surprised and indignant that his services should be so slighted, but Collingwood was not the man to be crushed by such a circumstance, or to make much noise about it. He felt it—felt it keenly; for he loved, as all brave men love, the honourable recognition of service when it is felt to have been well and fully earned. But, after all, this is the mere ephemera of fame, one of the accidents of real glory, not glory itself. Medals become forgotten; we no longer remember who had them and who had not: a title is no more than a sound; conferred distinctions expire; but the great deeds of a true-hearted hero outlive them all; they renew themselves from generation to generation and " blossom in the dust; " they have their roots deep down in the heart of the race; they are the property and possession of the afterworld, and do not depend for their ultimate glory on the fleeting honours of the moment. These may well be dispensed with where they are well deserved; for the right worthy hero is made illustrious, not by the honours bestowed upon him, but by the deeds that won them. Respect can add no grandeur to dignity itself, nor increase the honourableness of an unstained chivalry. Collingwood had no need of these to stamp the manhood which was within him with the seal of deserved acceptance; and though he liked the ornaments of his profession, which he was so well fitted to wear, yet he knew that these were of no value but as indications of true worth and desert. In our judgment of him we can afford to let these things go by now as entirely insignificant, looking to the personal weight and worth of him who did so much for his country, not only for the benefit of his own time but for that of posterity. They are nothing to us any longer beside so many virtues, so admirable and intrepid a behaviour.

Before leaving this epoch of Collingwood's life, let us dwell for a moment on the letter just quoted as exemplifying the warm heart of the gallant commander—the sweet homeward thoughts and tender reminiscences which, in the van of threatened danger, bring wife and child before him in happy visitation, and the storms of war are hushed in the whispers of domestic love—hushed with a quiet hope and a

murmured blessing. How full are these words of the
tenderness that sits so gracefully on a strong man,
which so worthily adorns a robust nature! No
effeminate cries or fears, no solemn charges got up
for the occasion, no noise or demonstration in the
face of peril so imminent; but the calm readiness of
a mind always prepared, of a life complete at any
moment, rounded and perfected in the fulfilment of
duty. What a great temperament must this be,
that can look at a life so ordered that it may be
resigned at any time without a sense of sacrifice or
regret; which asks for no supplement of days when
the summons comes, but like a good soldier is ready
at the first call, and never looks back! How do such
words show that in the midst of all his manly fearlessness his heart was elsewhere; with the loved
ones going to church on the quiet Sabbath morning!
But he was destined to hear a different peal than
that of the peaceful Sabbath bells, which might be
his death knell. Yes, that cannon thunder might
indeed sound his requiem. It might be that he
should see no more Sabbath mornings, and that the
next might plant a sharp thorn where the roses were
growing now, and fill the hearts he loved best with
heavy sighings and the bitterness of an irremediable
sorrow. But then the exigencies of the occasion
demanded his service. He could leave behind him
his blessing and a good name garlanded with

glorious deeds. He could bring to his country the inheritance of peace, and security to millions of households, for he knew he was not fighting against a shadow for a figment, but against a relentless and unscrupulous foe, who strove to subvert all the good ways of the world to make his own purposes triumphant; who sought to found a kingdom on the desolation of thousands of hearths, the ruin of households, the tears of widows and orphans, violating every principle of civil freedom and national independence in the greed which knew no satisfying, with a cruelty which knew no stayings of compunction or remorse.

No wonder that the name of Frenchman should at that time have been odious, as long as this cold-blooded arch-usurper sat upon his throne, surrounded by carnage, the rights and liberties of men trampled ruthlessly under foot. Collingwood well knew for what he was fighting and the stake at issue. He says in one of his letters :

" The question is not merely, who shall be conqueror, with the acquisition of some island or colony ceded by a treaty, and then the business concludes; but whether we shall any longer be a people,—whether Britain is still to be enrolled among the list of European nations, —whether the name of Englishman is to continue an appellation of honour, conveying the idea of every quality which makes human nature respectable, or a term of reproach and infamy, the designation of beggars and of slaves. Men of property must come forward with both purse and sword ; for the contest must decide whether they shall have anything, even a country, which they can call their own."

He thus speaks of Buonaparte in a letter to the Earl of Northesk in 1808:

"All the world may see Europe completely in the power of one man, whose ambition is unbounded, and who feels no restraint by any sentiment of honour, justice, or humanity. The humiliation of nations is his sport, and the fall of the greatest gives him the most exquisite delight: there is no distinction between friend and foe. Did not Portugal humble herself to him, and exhaust her treasure to purchase his forbearance? Has not Spain obeyed his nod, and been directed by him in all things? Is not Turkey crouching to him in the vain hope of warding off the impending ruin. It is a vain hope, for it is mankind of which he is the enemy ; it matters not what be the nation. England, alone, I feel, is superior to his utmost violence. Our insular situation gives us advantages which other nations had not, and I doubt not our resources, if wisely adminis- tered, will bear us through the storm."

It is difficult to conceive that one who had caused so much disaster to the human race should, when taken, have been allowed to live out a life replete with every comfort and convenience—and that at a risk of renewed outrages on society—only deprived of the name of liberty. It is one of those anomalies in the administration of justice which are perfectly incomprehensible to a thoughtful mind.   The murderer of an individual is punished with death, but the murderer of thousands, the defiler of every domestic relationship, and the violator of every civil, social, and religious institution is allowed to live in the most tolerable situation, is treated as a hero instead of a miscreant, and all this without shocking popular notions of justice and reparation; or even without exciting the abhorrence which deeds of infamy, accompanied by all the circumstances of licence and cruelty, merit, and ought naturally to inspire. Neither can we avoid the conclusion that it is due in a great measure to the mode in which the characters of freebooters and marauders on a large scale are regarded, and the false heroism with which they are popularly invested that their existence is rendered possible. It is owing to the delusive glamour thrown upon acts of violence, if of sufficient enormity and magnitude, and accompanied with qualities of daring and ingenuity, and to the heroic estimation in which their perpetrators are held by the traditions of the worst ages of barbarism that such pests of society and obstacles to civilization should ever obtain a hold or footing in the suffrages of mankind. It is thus that vicious principles are repaid upon the society which adopts or nurtures them, descending upon it like an awakened avalanche by the rule of a natural law of retribution. Just in proportion to the degree of our departure from a

correct interpretation of the principles of justice and
honesty, so far are we laying up in the society in
which we live all the evils which necessarily follow an
infraction of the moral law by force of which their
observance is made obligatory. The general standard
is lowered. Demoralization ensues. Cheating
implies to be cheated. The incendiary lights the
fires which eventually consume his own dwelling.
Stealing is repaid upon the thief by robbery. Lying
and treachery are inevitably followed by falsity and
deception. Thus it is that the monstrosity of a
Buonaparte may be directly charged to the warped
and contorted morality which allowed him to be
elevated to the rank of a hero. He was the mirror
in whom was reflected the collective perversions of
mankind in regard to national and political morality;
he was at once their focal embodiment and their
inexorable avenger.

In 1794, from the *Hector*, in which he held a
brief command, Collingwood removed to the *Excellent*, a 74-gun ship, in which he served many
years, and in which he consolidated a character and
reputation as one of the ablest commanders and
most upright and conscientious men in the English
navy. He and Nelson became still more intimate:
the terms of their friendship being so true, so
perfectly generous and unselfish as to be equally
creditable to both. Nelson generally commenced

his letters, "My dear Coll." Neither was Collingwood backward in expressing the same degree of
frank and manly affection.

Lord Collingwood now entered upon a long and
weary service : the blockading of Toulon. Seven
or eight months were spent in comparative inaction.
But soon the best energies of the fleet were called
out for a different occasion. On the 14th of
February, 1797, was fought the battle of St. Vincent,
when fifteen English ships of inferior force con-
tended with twenty-seven Spanish, seven of these
first-rate, not only winning the day, but carrying off
four prizes. Amongst the bravest and most prominent on this occasion was Captain Collingwood.
By whatever chivalrous conduct he was distinguished in 1794, it was now superseded and trans-
cended in a manner scarcely matched in the history
of brave and noble deeds. The "heart of oak"
indeed did good service and proved its genuine
toughness. Then England asserted herself: her
voice was not an empty sound, a tinkling cymbal,
but it rang through stolid plank and shroud and
rigging, through smoke and cannon-thunder till all
Europe reverberated the roar with a noise that
quelled the heart of tyranny and made the usurper
tremble to his footstool. During the night of the
13th the proximity of the enemy was announced by
their signal guns through a thick and heavy atmos-

phere, and when daylight appeared they were seen to be scattered widely apart, whilst the English fleet were all in a body. "We flew to them," says Collingwood, "as a hawk to his prey, passed through them in the disordered state in which they were, separated them into two distinct parts, and then tacked upon their largest division." Astonished at so much promptitude and daring, the enemy had not time to draw together before the battle began. "Here comes the *Excellent*," cried Nelson, as they closed to the fight, "which is as good as two added to our number;" and she soon shamed the praise in so signally transcending it. Collingwood's ship was amongst the first in action. He engaged the *San Salvadore del Mundo*, a first-rate of 112 guns. "We were not farther from her," says Collingwood, describing the engagement in a letter to his wife with one of those home touches which show where his heart was, "than the length of our garden." So hot was the fire that very soon her colours were hauled down, and Collingwood, understanding by signs from the signalman that she surrendered, "left her to be taken possession of by somebody behind, and made sail for the next." This happened to be the *San Isidro*, of 74 guns, of which he came close alongside. A raking fire brought down her colours also in ten minutes; but Collingwood, seeing the ship he had supposed to have struck again in action, with her flag up, not to be deceived a second time, made her hoist the British colours instead of her own, upon which she was taken in charge by a frigate. Then he hastened with all the sail he had left, at the most imminent risk, to the relief of Nelson, who was in a very awkward position under the fire of two of the largest Spanish ships, the *San Nicolas*, 80 guns, and *San Josef*, 112 guns. Ranging, close alongside the former, the *Excellent* poured into her a deluge of shot which actually passed through one vessel and into the other which lay on the other side of it. This he continued until his opponents were dumb; the fiery breath beaten quite out of them in the terrible encounter; and so he left them to be boarded by Nelson and his ship's crew, and driven at sword's point from deck to deck to a compelled surrender. But this was not all. Did his ship bear a charm of safety, or was it so animated by the brave spirit of its captain, as to make daring invulnerable, that, emulating the fabled heroes of old, he passed still to another ship, the *Santissima Trinidada*, the Spanish Admiral Cordova's ship, of 132 guns and four decks—"such a ship," says he, "as I never saw before,"—and with all the ardour of a new engagement fought her fiercely in the jaws of death for a long hour, and finally, with the assistance of some other ships which came up, almost annihilated her? At last, as night came down and fresh forces were poured upon the English, they retired, carrying with them the four ships which had surrendered.

"I am sure you will admire the fortitude and magnanimity of Sir John Jervis," says Collingwood, in writing to his father-in-law of this battle, "in determining to attack so superior a force; but should we not be grateful to him, who had such confidence in his fleet, that he thought no force too great for them? Though the different ships were differently circumstanced, and bore unequal shares in the action, all have the merit of having done their utmost."

Conduct so distinguished as that of Collingwood on this occasion could be no longer overlooked. Lord St. Vincent joined his name with the names of Trowbridge and Nelson in the praises of that day; whilst Nelson himself wrote gratefully, the day after the battle:

"My dearest friend: 'A friend in need is a friend indeed' was never more truly verified than by your most noble and gallant conduct yesterday in sparing the *Captain* from further loss; and I beg, both as a public officer and a friend, you will accept my most sincere thanks. I have not failed by letter to the Admiral to represent the eminent services of the *Excellent*. Tell me how you are; what are your disasters. I cannot tell you much of the *Captain's*, except by note of Captain Miller's, at two this morning; about sixty killed and wounded, masts bad, &c. We shall meet at Lagos; but I could not come near you without assuring you how sensible I am of your assistance in nearly a critical situation. Believe me, as ever, your most affectionate HORATIO NELSON."

Collingwood's reply was not a whit less hearty. It is dated from the *Excellent* on the same day, as follows :

" My dear good friend: First let me congratulate you on the success of yesterday—on the brilliancy it attached to the British Navy, and the humility it must cause to its enemies—and then let me congratulate my dear Commodore on the distinguished part which he ever takes when the honour and interests of his country are at stake. It added very much to the satisfaction which I felt in thumping the Spaniards, that I released you a little. The highest rewards are due to you and *Culloden:* you formed the plan of attack—we were only accessories to the Don's ruin; for, had they got on the other tack, they would have been sooner joined, and the business would have been less complete. We have come off pretty well considering: eleven killed and fourteen wounded. You saw the four-decker going off this morning to Cadiz: she should have come to Lagos to make the thing better, but we could not brace our yards to get nearer. I beg my compliments to Captain Martin: I think he was at Jamaica when we were. I am ever, my dear friend, affectionately yours, C. COLLINGWOOD."

"I will partake of nothing," says Nelson, very nobly, in a letter to his brother on this occasion, "but what shall include Collingwood and Trowbridge." In describing this engagement afterwards to the Duke of Clarence, Nelson says:

"At this time, the *Salvadore del Mundo* and *San Isidro* dropped astern, and were fired into in a masterly style by the *Excellent*, Captain Collingwood, who compelled the *San Isidro* to hoist English colours, and I thought the large ship, *Salvadore del Mundo*, had also struck; but Captain Collingwood, disdaining the parade of taking possession of beaten enemies, most gallantly pushed up, with every sail set, to save his old friend and messmate, who was to appearance in a critical state."

A generous letter from Admiral Waldegrave may be added to Collingwood's well-deserved testimonials on this occasion.

"My dear Collingwood: Although Dacres has in a great degree expressed all I feel on the subject, yet I cannot resist the satisfaction of telling you myself, that nothing, in my opinion, could exceed the spirit and true officership which you so happily displayed yesterday. Both the Admiral and Nelson join with me in this opinion; and nothing but ignorance can think otherwise. God bless you, my good friend; and may England long possess such men as yourself;—it is saying everything for her glory. Truly yours, WILLIAM WALDEGRAVE."

This indeed was no penny trumpet fame. It bore the stamp of a nation's gratitude and swelled through the civilized world. When he was offered a medal, in common with every other commander of the fleet, with a fine-spirited independence and just self-respect, he very properly refused it whilst that for Lord Howe's victory had been withheld from him. "I feel," said he to Lord St. Vincent, with a degree of emotion, but great firmness, "that I was then improperly passed over: and to receive such a distinction now, would be to acknowledge the propriety of that injustice." "That is precisely the answer which I expected from you, Captain Collingwood," was the reply. Both medals were afterwards transmitted to him, with a sort of apology for the detention of the former.

The Rev. J. S. Clarke, in summing up the life of Collingwood, says:

"It is due to the fame of Collingwood, to state that the gallantry and splendid instance of generous friendship which he exhibited in firing into the *San Nicolas* and *San Josef*, to relieve Nelson from the pressure of such adversaries, and then passing on in search of an antagonist for himself, stands out alone in the naval history of England."

An illustration of the difference of spirit prevailing in the English and French navies, and the degree of confidence with which it was regarded, may be shown by an extract from a French writer in the

Moniteur, of the 5th of November, 1793, a little more than three months before the engagement just described.   He says, "Unanimity and discipline reign amongst officers and men, and all burn with desire to fight the enemies of their country, to the very banks of the Thames and under the walls of London." A boast which seems to have had very little weight with the government, since it was decreed by the National Convention, that, "the captains and officers of any ship of the line, belonging to the republic, who should haul down the national colours to the vessels, however numerous, of an enemy, unless the French ship should be so shattered as to be in danger of sinking before the crew could be saved, should be pronounced traitors to their country and suffer death," and that any captains or officers who should surrender to a force double their own, unless under the before-mentioned circumstances, should suffer in the same manner.

If nations could be made brave by convention and courageous by act of parliament, then were fighting easy and victory secure.   But, unfortunately for such a system of hero-making, men claim for themselves the right of independence of action, and refuse to submit their deeds to the letter of prescription and the rule of the senate.   What a storm of rebellion would have been excited in the English fleet, from the first commander to the least and lowest of the service, if it had been thought necessary that the government of England should legislate for the courage of her defenders! What a tempest of indignation and protest would it have called forth! How degrading to the spirit of true bravery, how utterly superfluous and impertinent would it have been felt to have been; how entirely repugnant to the sentiments of every true-born Englishman! As a contrasting picture to this painful and derogatory circumstance, an anecdote is told of Lord Collingwood, which may be repeated here. "A young officer sent in charge of a convoy, with only a small force, applied to Collingwood to ask him what he must do in case he should meet the enemy. 'Let them sink *you*,' was the answer, 'and that will give the convoy time to escape.'" A reply which, one may be sure, would not require to be supplemented by act of parliament.

Again the note of war is suspended. Once more Collingwood writes to his father-in-law, in a strain of domestic tenderness, which shows how deep the springs of his being lay, how firm were the foundations of his life, and how little they depended on the world's honours and the world's rewards. It is dated, off Cadiz, May 22nd, 1797.

"I should have written to my dear Sarah on this her birthday; but as I wrote to her very lately, and have not yet thanked you for your kind letter, I shall send my congratulations and blessing to her, on this occasion, through you. Tell her, then, how sincerely, how constantly, I pray to heaven that she may see many happy returns of this day—that she may long live a source of joy to her husband, a blessing to her family, and an example of worth and goodness to all her sex. With the affection of such a wife, and the esteem and regard of her good and respectable family, I feel that I have nothing to ask to increase my happiness, but to see my country composed in peace. That will indeed be a happy day."

Now came another long period of inaction. Collingwood was appointed to watch the enemy's ships in the harbour of Cadiz. Month after month passed and found him in this monotonous situation.

At this time the English nation, and specially Ireland, discontented at the high taxation, the exorbitant price of provisions—the oppressive consequences of the war everywhere felt—and inflamed with a pervading dissatisfaction communicated from other nations in the struggle for liberty—or license under that name—manifested a revolutionary spirit which required all the policy of Pitt's government to control and repress. Nor did the social earthquake, which at that time shook all Europe, stop at the seaboard. The navy became largely disaffected, and mutiny showed its hydra-head in various parts of the British fleet. In the Mediterranean, off Spithead, and at the Nore, mutinies burst forth, and were

quelled, with difficulty, by the severest measures.
And yet, harshly as these outbreaks were treated,
they were not wholly unreasonable. Round-robins
had been addressed to the commander-in-chief,
setting forth the very real grievances of seamen, and
making requests for better pay, better food, better
attention to the sick, and, on a return from sea, permission for a short absence; all of which Lord Howe
disregarded. To man the navy during these severe
times impressment was in full force. Men were
carried off against their will, and forced either to
serve or find a substitute. To compel subjection to
so monstrous an infringement of liberty, the lash
was freely used; and, very often, in the hands of the
heartless and cruel, ¦ where it was not needed.
Criminals of the worst and vilest sort were taken
out of the prisons and sent to sea, who either corrupted others with disaffection or disgusted them
with their bad conduct. Again, some of the ships
were so ill-provisioned and watered, that they became no better than prisons of the worst description.
The crews were hardly allowed to leave their ships,
even when in port; and thus fomented discontent
and turbulence.

Perhaps there is nothing which shows the philosophic spirit more distinctively, than the inability to
be surprised by anything which may happen. Weak
persons are astonished at every obstacle or contrary

chance which may befall them.   Sickness, loss of friends or goods ; baseness or ingratitude in others ; faithlessness of relied securities; the hour of death ; all come upon them as something quite out of the course of life and nature.   They do not know how to support them, because they have never anticipated or made any preparation for them.   Whereas, he who is thoughtful and wise knows quite well that any of these may occur to him at any moment, and, however acutely he may feel them, he is not surprised by them.   They belong to the common round of being.   He knows this, and has, in a measure, provided for them and anticipated them ; so that when they do come, he knows how to act, to supply every remedy and make the best of the situation. Whatever else he may lose, he retains his presence of mind, and does not, like a bewildered child, run, aimlessly, hither and thither.   It was just so at this crisis with Lord Collingwood.   He had seen the tempest approaching; he knew it must come; he had furled his sails and dropped his anchor, metaphorically speaking ; so that while the whole continent of Europe, and a great part of the English nation, were suffering from the devastating storm which tore the social and political world, Collingwood's ship—the little world of the *Excellent*—was, perhaps, about the only place where it was unfelt in any active form.

And here one learns the value of a right and

reasonable government. Collingwood's rule was perfectly mild, and, at the same time, strictly uncompromising : a most judicious mixture of firmness and gentleness; and so well maintained was it that he would not allow the word "mutiny" to be heard on his ship. "Mutiny, sir, mutiny in my ship," he would say to an officer making such a charge. "If it can have arrived at that, it must be my fault, and the fault of every one of the officers. It is a charge of the gravest nature, and it shall be most gravely inquired into." This generally caused the affair to be regarded and passed over in a lighter manner. To severity of treatment Collingwood was a strong enemy ; and yet, strange to say, his rule was entirely efficacious. Such faith had Lord St. Vincent in Collingwood's government, that when there were any more than usually refractory and unmanageable spirits, he would say, "Send them to Collingwood, and he will bring them to order." This was accomplished for the most part without the use of severe physical means; but really by Collingwood's strength of will. There was no wavering or uncertainty about him. His resolution was of adamant; so that whoever came into close opposition to it must give way or be crushed. It was really a domination of reason, an illustration of the superiority of a rational over a material or brute force. He had a moral power so thorough, genuine, and well-supported, that it was irresistible. His determination to be obeyed was absolute; disobedience meant destruction : and this was so well understood, together with the real advantages of obedience, that it worked with the inevitableness of law. Retribution was swift, certain, and inexorable; so that a man knew rebellion was as certain of its consequences as putting his hand into flame would have been. He knew, at the same time, that a right course of conduct would ensure him the kindliest treatment and the greatest consideration; he thus had every inducement, compulsory and persuasive, to fulfil his duty. A circumstance. is told by his biographer, Mr. Newnham Collingwood, which confirms this :

"On one occasion, a seaman was sent from the *Romulus*, who had pointed one of the forecastle guns, shotted to the muzzle, at the quarter-deck, and standing by it with a match, declared that he would fire at the officers unless he received a promise that no punishment should be inflicted upon him. On his arrival on board the *Excellent*, Captain Collingwood, in the presence of many of the sailors, said to him with great sternness of manner : 'I know your character well, but beware how you attempt to excite insubordination in this ship; for I have such confidence in my men, that I am certain I shall hear in an hour of everything you are doing. If you behave well in future, I will treat you like the rest, nor notice here what happened in another ship; but if you endeavour to excite mutiny, mark me well, I will instantly head you up in a cask and throw you into the sea.' Under the treatment which he met with in the *Excellent,* this man became a good and obedient sailor, and never afterwards gave any cause of complaint."

At this time flogging was the commonest mode of punishment in the navy. It was used on the most trivial occasions, and was considered so much a matter of course, that a sailor was looked upon as " green," and laughed at by his messmates, who had never suffered under the lash. To give an idea of the enormous extent to which this was carried, an instance may be mentioned of a seaman on the *Zealous,* who was sentenced by court-martial to receive four hundred lashes with a cat-o'-nine-tails on his bare back for having uttered mutinous and seditious expressions and behaving with contempt to his superior officer. He was to be accompanied by a surgeon and to receive fifty lashes alongside of the *Zealous,* and thirty-five lashes alongside of ten other vessels. If he could not receive all at once, he was to be kept in custody and to receive the rest when able. Those who have seen the fearful instrument used on these occasions may form some idea of the nature of the punishment. Of course he did not submit to it all ; no mortal frame could have survived such an infliction. After suffering twice and being imprisoned for a length of time, the unexecuted part of the sentence was remitted by

Collingwood, who, one may be sure, would be sick at heart that such an occurrence should take place within his jurisdiction.

Collingwood resorted to flogging on his own ship as seldom as possible, and with the greatest un-willingness, and if, according to the mode of governing at that time, he was compelled to do so, it caused him much pain. For a long time after such a punishment had taken place he would not speak a word, and was sometimes silent a whole day after-wards. From a record of punishments inflicted on his ship (which he registered himself and used to ponder thoughtfully, though no account of punish-ment was officially required at that time) it appears that from May to September, 1793, twelve men suffered at different times from six to twelve lashes, never more, and always for serious offences, as disaffection, stealing, fighting, and riotous behaviour. His dislike to this mode of punishment so increased with experience, that in the latter part of his life more than a year often passed without his once resorting to it. "I cannot for the life of me," he once observed, "comprehend the religion of an officer who prays all one day and flogs his men all the next." One day, when his chief officer was standing by some men who were doing their work badly, he said, "I wish I were the Captain for your sakes." Presently Collingwood touched him on the shoulder and said, "And pray, Clavell, what would you have done if you had been Captain?" "I would have flogged them well, sir," was the reply. "No, you would not, Clavell; no, you would not," said Collingwood. "I know you better." If one of the midshipmen made a complaint of a sailor, and Collingwood could not consistently overlook it, he would sometimes order the man to be punished the next day, and in the meantime, calling the youth to him, would say that perhaps the fault might be partly his own, but that, in any case, it would be a painful thing to see a man so much older than himself disgraced and punished, and that he would think the better of his disposition if a request were made for the man's pardon when he should be brought for punishment, which, of course, was accordingly done, and the man discharged with a reprimand.

The punishments substituted for the lash by Collingwood I believe have now become general in the navy; such as removal from mess, watering the grog, and extra duty. The last consisted in the man under punishment being compelled to be at the beck and call of the whole ship's company for the most trifling service, besides being made the butt and laughing-stock of his messmates. So much was this punishment disliked, that sailors have been known to declare they would have much preferred

E

three dozen lashes than be subjected to it. Even the worst characters lived in dread of it, and were kept in check by its fear.

But it was not only by negative means that Collingwood commanded the esteem and regard of every man who served under him. The sick of his crew, even when he was an admiral, were visited by him daily, and served from his own table; and when convalescent, were confided to the care of the lieutenant of the morning watch, and brought to him every morning for inspection. The healthy condition of his ship was always a matter of great anxiety to him, and he used every means to maintain it; such as restricting the use of water between decks, airing the hammocks, and keeping up a circulation of air by means of stoves in hot climates. So successful was he in the result of his precautions, that once when at sea during a period of more than a year and a half without going into port, his sick list never numbered more than six, and generally not more than four. When off Toulon, in the early part of 1808, he writes with just pride, "I have been long at sea, have little to eat and scarcely a clean shirt; and often do I say, Happy lowly clown. Yet with all this seawork, never getting fresh beef nor a vegetable, I have not one sick man in my ship. Tell that to Doctor ——."

What, perhaps, contributed more than anything

else to the healthiness of his crew, was his constant endeavour to keep his men in good spirits and in a wholesome frame of mind. When they were upon slack duty, he did all he could to keep them from idleness by various occupations and amusements. He always spoke to his men without roughness or rudeness of language. "If you do not know a man's name," he would say to his officers, "call him 'sailor,' and not 'you-sir,' and such other appellations; they are offensive and improper." He was also careful never to give useless or harassing orders, or to exact superfluous service.

All this was fully appreciated by his crew. The hardiest was not impervious to treatment so just and reasonable. Whenever he changed his ship, many a horny hand was drawn over eyes filled with drops of sorrow at his departure; for he obtained the name and held the character of "father" to his crew.

He took great pains in the training of his midshipmen, examining them personally once a week, and saying that nothing would give him greater pain than that they should not be able to pass. "Young —— appears to me," he says in one of his letters, "to be a very good, mild-tempered boy, and I will leave nothing undone which is in my power to promote his knowledge and interests. He is studying geometry with me, and I keep him close to his books. It is a pity, as he was intended for the sea-service

that he was not taught navigation; but I will, at
least, prepare him for a better master." The same
care was taken of the interests of his lieutenants. " I
stand between them and danger," he says, "as much
as I can ; but they have still, unfortunately, the
power to ruin themselves." His conduct to his
officers was uniformly polite and courteous; but as
no failure in duty was ever unobserved, so it was
never passed over in silence. His reproofs were conveyed directly, and were always dreaded. Once,
when in a hurry to complete the bread stores of his
ship, he asked the captain, an esteemed officer, if all
the boats had been despatched. The captain
replied that all had been sent with the exception of
his own barge. " Oh! of course," said the admiral,
"a captain's barge must never be employed for such
purposes ; but I hope they will make every possible
use of mine."

Lord Collingwood had an intimate and exact
knowledge of all the technicalities of his profession.
He was a terror to the idle and slovenly ; for he
insisted upon everything being done rightly, and
could himself splice a rope or perform any other
office of the ship with as much dexterity as a common
seaman. He could detect in a moment anything
which was wrong, or out of place, and a sailor's
neglect was always reprimanded with few and not
strong words, but firmly and decisively. He once

undertook some extensive repairs of his ship whilst still at sea, and within sight of the port of the enemy. He could instruct the carpenter to the minutest detail, and was, indeed, as much at home in any minor operation of the service, as he was in the conduct of a fleet.

To his superiors in office, he knew how to protest when occasion required. Once, when off Cadiz, his vessel was signalled to weigh and to close with the admiral's ship. After she had been directed to alter her course five or six times, a lieutenant was asked for. In complying, Collingwood had his own boat manned and went also. As he walked the deck with Lord St. Vincent and Sir Robert Calder, he was handed an order for two bags of onions. "Bless me," said he, "is this the service, my lord? is this the service, Sir Robert? Has the *Excellent's* signal been made five or six times for two bags of onions? Man my boat, sir, and let us go on board again." And, although repeatedly pressed to stay for dinner, he refused to do so.

Amongst those anomalous obliquities which characterize popular morality, perhaps there is none more remarkable than the different manner which prevails of regarding public money from that of a private purse. It is thought no degradation to accept public money, though unearned. Neither in spending it is there a better code. It would be curious if it were possible to know at how much less cost our national institutions would be maintained in the same degree of efficiency if every person who disbursed money towards their support had first to earn it. I suppose that the generality of persons in such a situation would disdain a problem of this kind. And yet there is one instance, at least, on record, in which the question is answered by individual testimony very satisfactorily and indisputably. Collingwood felt his nation's misfortunes from a personal point of view, and used its money and property exactly as if they had been his own; writing to Sir James Saumarez, he says :—

"I am really at a loss to know whether the enemy will make a push in the dark nights, or have adopted a policy slower in its operation, but more certain; and mean to stay in port till our ships are worn out at sea, and the expense of keeping them there has brought the finances of the country to poverty and exhaustion. This is a condition to be as carefully guarded against as a present invasion, for the latter will be the certain consequences of the former, if ever we are unhappily reduced to it. Strongly impressed with this belief, my thoughts are ever bent on economising, and doing all in my power to lessen the expense of sailing the ships. The difference I observe in them is immense; some men, who have the foresight to discern what our [first difficulties will be, support and provide their ships as by enchantment, one scarce knows how; while others, less provident, would exhaust a dock-yard, and still be in want. I do not think those gentlemen should go to sea; they certainly do not regard or feel for the future necessities of their country."

So careful was Lord Collingwood of the public purse, that the whole charge for extraordinary disbursements during the five years when he had the command of the Mediterranean fleet, including a mission to Morocco for horses, postage of letters, &c., &c., only amounted to fifty-four pounds. It is needless to say that he was always most scrupulous in rendering an exact account of his private property chargeable with income-tax.

His endeavours to promote economy in the stores and furniture of the service are exemplified in a letter to a captain in his fleet, which I extract from one of his unpublished books of Orders, &c. It is as follows :—

"Observing in your journal of the 14th of March last, when clearing for action, a number of casks and arm-chests were thrown overboard, which I apprehend must have proceeded from not having made a proper arrangement and stowage of those stores, which were never intended to be thrown into the sea, but for the use and service of his Majesty's ship :—

"In the course of your short voyage there has been more masts, sails, and rigging lost than in all the squadron besides, and far beyond proportionate to the service you had to perform :—

"I must desire you will be more provident and careful

of the masts and furniture in future, and take care
that the stores and casks are at all times so stowed that
it may not be necessary to throw even a bucket overboard when you prepare for action."   .

In the middle of the Battle of St. Vincent, Collingwood was heard to exclaim to his boatswain, " Bless
me, Mr. Peffers, how came we to forget to bend our
old top-sail? They will quite ruin that new one : it
will never be worth a farthing again."

Lord Collingwood had so large a faith in the
power of a reasonable education, that he believed
" stupidity itself might be instructed;" so that
with such a creed there was no excuse for
ignorance. But how much must his patience have
been tried to find it rampant everywhere around
him. Incompetency and incapability were so common in the fleet, that some of the appointments
made by the government at home had, for those
reasons, to be refused or protested against. " I have
got my commander's commission," said a lieutenant,
after an interview with Lord Chatham at the
Admiralty, " but Lord Chatham told me, it was not
for any merit of my own, but from the powerful
interest of my friends." What made such appointments as these the more flagrant was that there
were numbers of able and deserving officers in the
service who awaited promotion in vain. Indeed, so
disgusted were many of these with the venality

practised in appointments of this sort, that they left the service altogether.

"That officer," said Collingwood, on one occasion, of one of these scions of private patronage, "should never sail without a store-ship in company. He knows as much seamanship as the King's Attorney-General : I would not trust him with a boat in a trout-stream."

At another time, he said of a young officer, "He is living on the navy, not serving in it."

Again, he writes to Mr. Blackett in 1809 :—

"I am surprised to see Mr. —— come out again. They think, when they have served six years at sea, they should be made lieutenants, and never deem it necessary to qualify themselves. He is a good, quiet young man, and walks about doing no harm, but he has no activity in him. Such people become rather pensioners upon the navy than officers in it."

Of course, such a condition of things as this was a great detriment to the fleet, as well as a source of the greatest annoyance to those who had the welfare of the service at heart—to say nothing of the incalculable extra trouble involved. For one of the worst evils of a defection of duty is that it does not terminate with itself, but also, directly or indirectly, produces a dead-lock in the whole mechanism of order. By a want of punctuality or observance in another I am compromised myself, and every one with whom I am connected in affairs. It is like throwing a stone into

a pond: one wave begets another until the whole
surface is broken. Though there be but one stone,
there are a hundred ripples produced from it.
There is really no telling where the ill results
of a failure in duty may end; for it not only acts
dynamically on other duties and persons, but, by the
viciousness of bad example, its influence may be
positively interminable. A mischievous or dishonest act is the first spark of an incendiary, and
would, if allowed its full and legitimate effects and
consequences, inflame and corrupt a commonwealth.

The dissatisfaction caused by arbitrary advance-
ments rose to the higher ranks of the service in 1798,
when Nelson, a junior in the fleet, was promoted to
command the expedition to the coast of Egypt, which
resulted in the Battle of the Nile; several senior
admirals having been passed over who had signalized
themselves as men of gallantry and ability. The
discontent prevailed to such an extent, that the
admirals and captains were forbidden by the commander-in-chief to entertain each other at table; a
great privation at that time, the fleet being stationed
off Cadiz during a long and monotonous blockade of
that port. It was a season of bitter disappointment,
too, to Collingwood for other reasons, though he said
little about it. When Nelson was appointed to the
much-coveted service, Collingwood had evidently
hoped that he might have been asked to join it; and

very reasonably so; for was not he one of Nelson's oldest friends, from whom he had received the strongest protestations of affection and friendship? Nelson would, of course, have a voice in the selection of those who should bear him company, if it did not wholly depend upon his choice. Who so fit as his old friend, whose bravery was beyond impeachment, whose judgment was the soundest, who might be depended upon with the most implicit confidence? Nelson knew that of all the desires which could possess the heart of his tried friend and colleague, this would be the strongest; that of all which he had in his power to bestow upon him, this would give him the greatest satisfaction. But, from whatever motive or reason, and Collingwood never for a moment suspected an interested one, though some of his most friendly biographers have not hesitated to do so, Nelson went without him—quite overlooked him. Nelson went to a great battle and obtained a victory which wreathed his brows with fresh laurels and gained him the acclamations of applausive millions: but, in my judgment, that heroically-hearted comrade of his, whom he left waging a paltry war against the poor cabbage-carriers of St. Lucar, who never once breathed a suspicion of the true faith of his friend, and evidently allowed himself to feel none, who sent nothing but the best and warmest wishes of his heart after him, who measured the

actions of his brother by the grand standard by
which himself was ruled, fought a greater battle and
achieved a nobler victory. In the Great Book in
which those high deeds are recorded which do not
enter the category of human praise, that name will
assuredly not be written second.

Of all that is touching in sentiment and beautiful
in the expression of it, I do not know anything more
so than this letter, which Collingwood wrote, shortly
after the battle, to his friend Captain Ball. It is dated
on the *Excellent*, still off Cadiz, October 28, 1798.

"I cannot express to you how great my joy was
when the news arrived of the complete and unparalleled
victory which you have obtained over the French, or
what were my emotions of thankfulness, that the life of
my worthy and much respected friend was preserved,
through such a day of danger, to his family and his
country. I congratulate you, my dear friend, on your
success. Oh, my dear Ball, how I have lamented that
I was not one of you! Many a victory has been won,
and I hope many are yet to come, but there never has
been, nor will be, perhaps, again, one in which the fruits
have been so completely gathered, the blow so nobly
followed up, and the consequences so fairly brought to
account. I have been almost broken-hearted all the
summer. My ship was in as perfect order for any
service as those which were sent; in zeal I will yield
to none; and my friendship—my love for your admirable admiral, gave me a particular interest in serving
with him. I saw them preparing to leave us, and to

leave me, with pain; but our good chief found employment for me, and, to occupy my mind, sent me to cruise
off St. Lucar, to intercept the market-boats, the poor
cabbage-carriers. Oh, humiliation! But for the consciousness that I did not deserve degradation from any
hand, and that my estimation would not be depreciated
in the minds of honourable men, I should have died
with indignation. I am tired of it; and you will
believe that I am glad that to-morrow I depart for
England."

Deserving no less terms of praise is his letter to
Nelson, on the same occasion.

"I cannot, my dear friend, express how great my joy is,
for the complete and glorious victory you have obtained
over the French, the most decisive, and, in its consequences, perhaps, the most important to Europe that was
ever won; and my heart overflows with thankfulness to
the Divine Providence for His protection of you through
the great dangers which are ever attendant on services
of such eminence. So total an overthrow of their fleet,
and the consequent deplorable situation of the army
they have in Africa, will, I hope, teach those tyrants in
the Directory a lesson of humility, and dispose them to
peace and justice, that they may restore to those states
which they have ruined, all that can now be saved
from the wreck of a subverted government and plun-
dered people. I lament most sincerely the death of
Captain Westcott; he was a good officer and a worthy
man; but if it were a part of our condition to choose a
day on which to die, where could we have found one so
memorable, so eminently distinguished among great

days?   I have been here, miserable enough, all the
summer: but I hope to go to England very soon.   The
Barfleur, Northumberland, and some other ships, are expected to relieve the old ones.   Say to Lady Nelson,
when you write to her, how much I congratulate her
on the safety, honours, and services of her husband.
Good God! what must be her feelings!   How great her
gratitude to heaven for such mercies!   Pray give my
hearty congratulations to all my friends in your fleet.
I am glad to understand that my worthy Ball and
Darby are recovering.   That success may ever attend
you, is the constant prayer of your faithful and affectionate friend."

Collingwood's care of his men, during the tedious
blockade of Cadiz, was of the most praiseworthy
kind.   Day after day passed in eventless tedium.
To keep a crew of 800 men in health and spirits,
during such a service, at a time of prevalent
disaffection, was a matter of extreme difficulty.
Indeed, it is no wonder that his own should have been
severely tried.   He encouraged his men to compose
a band with instruments of their own making, so
that on the bright moonlit nights of the soft southern
climate, the deck resounded with their music and
re-echoed to the mirth of dancing and singing.   Then
the rats devoured the bagpipes, and a raid of exter-
mination was made upon them; no doubt, much to
the advantage of the ship's stores.   "It has always
been a maxim with me," he says, in one of his letters

from this station, "to engage and occupy my men, and to take such care for them that they should have nothing to think of beyond the current business of the day." Thus, whilst the mind of the brave captain was oppressed by a thousand cares, of which that resulting from inaction was not the least weighty, he strove to distribute smiles around him, and to diffuse as much content and satisfaction as the circumstances of the situation would allow.

But not inglorious could such a rest be. In the heart of the great commander the old fires were yet alive. He stood ready and watchful. It is only to the idle in spirit that inaction is a curse. "They also serve who only stand and wait." Not only was intercourse forbidden to the commanders of the fleet, at this time, but a great many other annoyances were imposed. Collingwood thus writes to his father-in-law at this disorganised period :—

"They all complain that they are appointed to many unworthy services, and I have my share with the rest; but I place myself beyond the reach of such matters; for I do them with all the exactness in my power, as if they were things of the utmost importance, though I do not conceal what I think of them. In short, I do as everybody does—wish myself at home very much."

What a very noble lesson may here be learnt from Collingwood's behaviour under these circumstances!

Instead of allowing these trying services to irritate and rankle in his mind, he disarmed their power of disturbing him by simply despatching them at once. Useful or useless, willingly or unwillingly, he knew they must be done; he therefore took care not to waste his time and weaken his energy by complaint, but laid all bitterness and annoyance stingless at his feet by their unhesitating fulfilment.

It is impossible not to be impressed with the grand sense of Duty which filled the hearts of the best men of this time. "England expects that every man will do his duty," was typical of the reigning sentiment of the British service. But Collingwood interpreted the term at a higher rate and gave it a still grander significance. He had a loftier rule than England's "expectation" for doing his duty. He had an authoritative code which could not be transmitted by a ship's signals, nor even by electric wire. It was written on his heart, and burned in golden letters there. It was his pillar of cloud by day and his beacon of fire by night. Duty was to him the noblest function of his soul, the life-spring and fountain of his being.

Are you one of those who are fighting through life darkly; to whom labour is hard, and the fruits far off or not at all visible? Do you know the aching weariness? Has the iron entered into your soul? Do you ask yourself every day, Why was I born to a lot so severe, or, indeed, why was I born at all? I can set before you something which shall be as balm to your mind, as an anodyne to your spirit. Are you poor, despised, of no account amongst men? I will point out to you the way to true nobility. Are you weak and powerless, depressed with your feebleness as an instrument in the universe? I will show how you may be strong in the invincible security of a citadel which cannot be shaken. It is that you do your duty; that you fulfil all that is given you to do in the most sacred, complete and conscientious manner. To be honest, upright, earnest in the least thing, is to be concerned in the social progress of the whole human race. It is the one thing required of you. It shall attach you to the army of God and make you an instrument in the purposes of the Eternal. Whatever else other men do or do not, these are your riches, these are your heritage, these are your patent right and title to the truest nobility: to possess your soul in integrity, honour and honesty, and to have faith in consecrating yourself to a pure, energetic and disinterested course of action; unflinching, unrelaxing, undespairing. The consciousness of having done your duty, fulfilled your destiny, and increased your one talent to ten, a hundred, or a thousand talents, shall fill your soul with an enlarged joy, a living and abundant fountain of peace, a solid satisfaction which neither wealth

F

nor the world's praise can bestow, nor the black
wing of death cover to your shame.

In the midst of much pain and heart-sickness,
Collingwood at last obtained a relief from his too
arduous services. His ship, ordered home for repairs,
was paid off, and he returned once more to his quiet
home at Morpeth. But not long was he suffered to
enjoy a respite from professional service. In about
three months we find him once more at sea.

His letters at this time breathe a tenderness of
feeling, a warmth of affection, a deploring of the
necessity of war and a longing for peace, united at
the same time with the most unflinching adherence
to duty, at once creditable to him as a man, and
honourable to him as the patriotic servant and
defender of his country.

He writes to Mr. Blackett from the *Barfleur*, at
Torbay, on the 23rd of May, 1800:—

"Would to God that this war were happily con-
cluded! It is anguish enough to me to be thus for ever
separated from my family: but that my Sarah should,
in my absence, be suffering from illness is complete
misery. Pray, my dear sir, have the goodness to write
a line or two very often, to tell me how she does. I
am quite pleased at the account you give me of my
girls. If it were peace I do not think there would be
a happier set of creatures in Northumberland than we
should be."

Again, when lying off Brest, he writes, three

months afterwards, giving some account of the discomforts of his situation :—

"I do assure you when I reflect on my long absence from all that can make me happy, it is very painful to me, and what day is there that I do not lament the continuance of this war? We are wandering before this port with no prospect of change for the better. Nothing good can happen to us short of a peace. Every officer and man in the fleet is impatient for release from a situation which daily becomes more irksome to all. I see disgust growing round me very fast. Instead of softening the rigours of a service which must, from its nature, be attended with many anxieties, painful watchings, and deprivation of everything like comfort, a contrary system is pursued, which has not extended to me, but I see its effects on others and deplore them. What I feel as a great misfortune is, that there is no exercise of the military part of the duty, no practice of those movements by a facility in which one fleet is made superior to another. Whoever comes here ignorant in those points must remain so; for he will find other employment, about blankets and pigsties and tumbling provisions out of one ship into another. How the times are changed! Once when officers met, the first question was, What news of the French: is there any prospect of their coming to sea? Now there is no solicitude on the subject, and the hope of peace alone engages the attention of everybody.".

On the 4th of October he writes in a still more decided strain. His appeal for forbearance towards

his own character reaches the feelings, as indicative
of the humility of a sensitive and conscientious
nature. He had felt the long, hard struggle, the
struggle to keep up the best elements and faculties
of the soul intact, amidst all that was calculated to
strain them to the uttermost. Within and without
a great battle had to be fought continually. Every
moment brought its trials to such a mind as his,
and inaugurated a fresh warfare.

"It is a great comfort to me," he says, " banished, as I
am, from all that is dear to me, to learn that my beloved
Sarah and her girls are well. Would to heaven it were
peace, that I might come, and for the rest of my life be
blessed in their affection. Indeed, this unremitting
hard service is a great sacrifice, giving up all that is
pleasurable to the soul or soothing to the mind, and
engaging in a constant contest with the elements, or
with tempers and dispositions as boisterous and in-
tractable. Great allowance should be made for us when
we come on shore; for, being long in habits of absolute
command, we grow impatient of contradiction, and are
unfitted for the gentle intercourse of quiet life. I am
really in great hopes that it will not be long before the
experiment will be made upon me, for I think we shall
soon have peace; and, I assure you, that I will endeavour to conduct myself with as much moderation as
possible. I have come to another resolution, which is,
when this war is happily terminated, to think no more
of ships, but pass the rest of my days in the bosom of
my family, where, I think, my prospects of happiness
are equal to any man's."

I cannot omit his next letter to his father-in-law, for its strain of manly warmth, and the beautiful expression which it contains of the most elevated sentiments. It is dated from Plymouth Dock, December 27th, 1800:—

"I intend that you shall receive this on the 1st of January, your birthday; and I pray God that you may live to receive my congratulations, on the same occasion, for many years to come; that you may find in your family all the blessings which your paternal care of them has so justly merited, and filial piety can bestow; that you may long see your own good heart reflected in the kind and benevolent manners of your daughters; and that, in due time, my precious children may join their efforts in administering to your comfort. May you, my dear sir, be very happy; and, when better times come, may we all be glad together, and talk over this my long separation from all that is happiness, as a bondage and a peril that are past.

"I am here, conducting the fitting out of our fleet, which is, I assure you, a laborious office, but that I do not mind; and have now been near a month in port. What a month it would have been had my wife been with me! It grieves me ten times more than if I had been at sea."

One letter more, at this period, shall be given as further illustrative of Collingwood's character, and the generous breadth and disinterestedness of his nature. It is written to Mr. Blackett, from Cawsand Bay, near Plymouth, on the 18th of January, 1801.

"I have been a long time here, and do not know when I shall remove. It has been a melancholy, forlorn time to me; and I have not been quite well. There is a dreadful languor which I cannot shake off; but when Sarah comes, when I see her, I shall then be well. I do not write to her, because I think it likely they are now on their journey southward. Shall we ever have peace? I confess I do not expect to see it. All Europe has combined to reduce the power and annihilate the glory of England; but the stand we will make will be that of the lion at the mouth of his cave. I do not wish to see the honour of our country faded, or its interests injured; nor do I think it probable that I shall. The Danes and Swedes have joined the coalition, and we now seize them all.

"You have been made happy this winter in the visit from your daughter. How glad should I have been could I have joined you! But it will not be long; two years more, will, I think, exhaust me completely, and then I shall be fit only to be nursed. God knows how little claim I have on anybody to take that trouble. My daughters can never be to me what yours have been, whose affections have been nurtured by daily acts of kindness. They may be told that it is a duty to regard me, but it is not reasonable to expect that they should have the same feeling for a person of whom they have only heard; but, if they are good and virtuous, as I hope, and believe, they will be, I may share, at least, in their kindness with the rest of the world."

It added not a little to the sadness of these depressing seasons that Collingwood was frequently close to the English shore, and yet was separated from what he valued most there. In the later days of steam and telegraph, many a brief solace would have been snatched by the sight of the loved ones, which, at that period of long and toilsome journeying, was impossible. It was, as Collingwood says, much more trying than being at sea. At last, however, fortune favoured him with a much-desired meeting with his wife and one of his children. Expecting to remain some length of time in Cawsand Bay, he sent for his wife to join him there. Anticipating her visit, he writes, "I am delighted at the thought of seeing her soon, and it has cured me of all my complaints; indeed, I believe the cause of them was vexation and sorrow at being, as it were, lost to my family." But, at the moment when he thought his happiness complete, it had been almost snatched from him; for, just when he was expecting her arrival, an order came for him to go to sea as soon as possible. Already he was prepared to forego the meeting, having only been prevented from immediate departure by the duty of attending a court-martial, when Nelson wrote him a note, with the request that he would dine with him on shore that night, and delay his departure till the following morning. As they sat down to dinner, his wife and child were announced. "I flew to the inn," he says, "where I had desired my wife to come, and found her and little Sarah as well after their journey as if it had lasted only for the day. No greater happiness is human nature capable of than was mine that evening; but at dawn we parted, and I went to sea." "How surprised you would have been," he wrote, afterwards, to Mrs. Moutray, "to have popped into the Fountain inn, and seen Lord Nelson, my wife, and myself, sitting by the fireside cosing, and little Sarah teaching Phillis, her dog, to dance:"— a delightful picture, sketched by the masterful stroke of a sympathetic pen, as only an Englishman with English tastes and feelings could sketch it. Too short and sweet it was, and sadly remembered.

"You will have heard from Sarah," he wrote to Mr. Blackett, "what a meeting we had, how short our interview, and how suddenly we parted. It is a grief to me to think of it now: it almost broke my heart then. After such a journey, to see me but for a few hours, with scarce time for her to relate the incidents of her journey, and no time for me to tell her half that my heart felt at such a proof of her affection; but I am thankful that I did see her and my sweet child. It was a blessing to me, and composed my mind, which was before much agitated."

If we would arrive at a just idea of the sacrifices Collingwood was making at this time to his country, we must remember that all the natural current of his being was set against the sea and the kind of life which it demanded of him. To Nelson and others the life of adventure, the change of place, the

calls upon the animal energies, the very precarious-
ness and uncertainty of the morrow, may have given,
and no doubt did give, a zest to danger, and communicated a hopeful liveliness to inactivity. With
Collingwood it was otherwise. Every moment was
to him a sacrifice; for his sympathies lay in quite
other directions. He never loved the sea. "Pray
tell me," he writes to his wife, "all you can think
about our family and about the beauties of your
domain: the oaks, the woodlands and the verdant
meads." And writing to his father-in-law from the
Dardanelles, in 1807, he says, "Tell Sarah that I
hope she will have a comfortable house for me when
I come home. The farther it is from the sea-shore,
the less we shall be annoyed." "I shall go home,"
he says in 1808, "as soon as I can, and never after
have anything to do with ships." The love of glory
which with Nelson was a mastering passion, was with
Collingwood supplanted by a strong sense of duty
and necessity, which bore him manfully through a
life otherwise uncongenial to him. His mind was continually turning to home scenes, home enjoyments,
the education of his children, the cultivation of his
garden, a philosophic life of intellectual culture and
repose, the exercise of beneficence, the fostering of
the highest virtues, despising wealth as the object
of existence, and disdaining every empty ambition.
We may easily understand, as the autumn of life

approached and his frame lost its elasticity, that he should suffer fits of depression from which he was only aroused by the calls of his office. " I am an object of your pity," he says to his old friend Mrs. Moutray, with pathetic sadness, "yet cease not to love me."

In April of the same year, 1801, the spring of his hopes strewed his soul with fresh blossoms of joy in the prospect of a new peace; but they were born of the fickleness of the season, only to be withered. His letter upon this occasion teems with delightful anticipation. It is addressed to Mr. Blackett :—

" I can still talk to you of nothing but the delight I experienced in the little I have had of the company of my beloved wife and of my little Sarah. What comfort is promised to me in the affections of that child, if it should please God that we ever again return to the quiet domestic cares of peace! I had written thus far when the account reached me of the action at Copenhagen, with the destruction of the Danish fleet, the death of that poor distracted Paul and its consequences. This success has almost turned my head with joy. Now I hope we shall have peace. God Almighty has prospered our arms; and I trust that it is the justice of our cause and the confidence with which we repose in Him, that have brought these blessings on us. I should be much obliged if you would send Scott a guinea for me, for these hard times must pinch the poor old man, and he will miss my wife, who was very kind to him."

Good man! how was his heart filled with happy

anticipations at this time, and how were they doomed to be disappointed! on the 9th of May, 1802, he writes:—

"I have at last got from my ship, and am safely landed. As the time approaches when I shall get home to my blessings, my impatience increases, and I can scarce persuade myself that I have now only to study how to make everybody about me as happy as they can be, and that every day will be that which I have been wishing for those ten years past. I am indeed feeling a degree of contentment which is truly pleasurable."

These were delusive promises; but the evil hour was delayed. The political sky became clearer. The demon of war folded his funereal pinions, sheathed his sword of flame, rolled up his dark banner, and prepared to depart, as the angel of peace, with welcome countenance, smiled from heaven and waved her olive branch triumphantly. Peace was signed at Amiens. The troubler of mankind had stayed his thirst for blood, and was supposed to be firmly seated on his consular throne. Thus the almost worn-out admiral was enabled to retire to his much-desired home.

His residence was at Morpeth, on the banks of the Wansbeck, in a beautiful situation. The elder of his two daughters was at this time eleven and the younger ten years of age. Collingwood was not one of those restless and ambitious spirits to whom the

gratification of their desire brings dissatisfaction.
With the prescience of every philosophic mind, he
knew the breadth and compass of his nature and
its requirements. The leisure he coveted did not
hang heavily on his hands. The home he had so
long wished for did not pall upon him, but grew
more dear to him every day; for every day found
full, earnest occupation of the most congenial and
wholesome sort. He had earned repose; but idleness was far from him. There were the '*Nelson*'
potatoes and large cabbages to be grown. But,
before everything else in his garden, his oaks
claimed his special attention. Of these he had
planted a nursery. He says in a letter to Lord
Radstock, some years later:—

"What I am most anxious about is the plantation
of oak in the country. We shall never cease to be a
great people while we have ships, which we cannot
have without timber; and that is not planted, because
people are unable to play at cards next year with the
produce of it. I plant an oak whenever I have a place to
put it in, and have some very nice plantations coming
on; and not only that, but I have a nursery in my
garden, from which I give trees to any gentleman who
will plant them, and instruction how to top them at a
certain age, to make them spread to knee timber."

These oaks were his pet care, and their growth one
of his particular anxieties. He said, if country gentlemen did not plant oaks our navy must depend upon

captures from the enemy, as there was at that time
difficulty in getting the necessary material. His
oaks were mentioned in his letters over and over
again. When off Cadiz, at the end of the year
1806, he writes to Lady Collingwood:—

"It is very agreeable to me to hear that you are
taking care of my oaks, and transplanting them to
Hethpoole. If ever I get back I will plant a good deal
there in patches; but before that can happen you and
I shall be in the churchyard, planted under some old
yew tree."

How little, in this consideration for posterity, did
he foresee the changes which a single generation
would effect; the iron coursers which should stem
the ocean, and fetch the produce of the remotest
corners of the globe; the time when to traverse half
a hemisphere would be but the pleasure trip of a
summer's holiday, when the great mass of human
labour, nay, the office of the winds and tides themselves, should be delegated to the giants of mechanism
and the force of steam!

One day an admiral whom he knew came to see
him, and found him digging industriously at the
bottom of a trench with old Scott, the gardener.
Old Scott was evidently a character. No doubt he
belonged to the family and considered himself a
part of it. One can imagine the respect which he
would entertain towards his master as the illustrious

sea commander, and the indulgent toleration with
which he would regard his accomplishments as
a gardener : the wondering interest with which he
would listen to scraps of narrative of sea-adventure,
his common sense questions and observations, the
relish with which he would retail any such scraps,
and the delight he would have in seeing the rapt
attention with which they were received by gossip-
ing neighbours. Then there were studies to be
followed ; for Collingwood, like every other accomplished man, never ceased learning. He made
draughts from favourite books, using largely that
most valuable instrument of culture, the taking of
abstracts and digests from what he read. It was
perhaps owing to this habit in some measure that
he attained the rare condensation of style and finish
of expression which so distinctively mark the fruits
of his pen.   He was a good historical scholar,
and had a well-read acquaintanceship with general
literature. He was also fond of drawing. But that
which occupied his mind and attention above all
other things, was the education of his daughters.
This was always a matter of the nearest interest to
him, and he never in his busiest moments lost sight
of its importance.   I will string together a few
extracts from several letters written at various times,
giving his views on this subject :—

  " My chief anxiety now is to see my daughters well

and virtuously educated, and I shall never think anything too good for them if they are wise and good
tempered. Tell them, with my blessing, that I am
much obliged to them for weeding my oaks. . . How
do my darlings go on? I wish you would make them
write to me by turns, and give me the whole history
of their proceedings. Oh! how I shall rejoice when I
come home to find them as much improved in knowledge
as I have advanced them in station in the world; but
take care they do not give themselves foolish airs.
Their excellence should be in knowledge, in virtue, and
benevolence to all; but most to those who are humble
and require their aid. This is true nobility, and is now
become an incumbent duty on them. . . I am anxious
about my children, now their governess is gone. I
beseech you, dearest Sarah, I beseech you keep them
constantly employed; make them read to you, not
trifles, but history, in the manner we used to do in the
winter evenings : blessed evenings, indeed ! The human
mind will improve itself if it be kept in action; but
grows dull and torpid when left to slumber. . . It
is impossible that at this distance I can direct and
manage the education of my daughters; but it costs
me many an anxious hour. The ornamental part of
education, though necessary, is secondary; and I wish
to see their minds enlarged by a true knowledge of
good and evil, that they may be able to enjoy the one
if it be happily their lot, and submit contentedly to
any fortune rather than descend to the other. . . It is
a great satisfaction to me that my daughters will
probably be educated well, and taught to depend upon
themselves for their happiness in this world; for if
their hearts be good, they have both of them heads

wise enough to distinguish between right and wrong. While they have resolution to follow what their hearts dictate, they may be uneasy under the adventitious misfortunes which may happen to them, but never unhappy; for they will still have the consolation of a virtuous mind to resort to. I am most afraid of outward adornment being made a principal study, and the furniture within being rubbish. What they call fashionable accomplishments, is but too often teaching poor misses to look bold and forward, in spite of a natural disposition to gentleness and virtue."

Such extracts as these might be largely added to. He desired that his elder daughter should keep a diary, noting events and adding comments upon them, which, he said, would be more valuable to him than all the books in Chirton library. He had the greatest dislike that his daughters should be made into "fine ladies." "Give them," he says to his wife, "a knowledge of the world which they have to live in, that they may take care of themselves when you and I are in heaven." He requested that they should "do everything for themselves;" and not read novels whilst young; but history, travels, essays, and Shakespeare's plays, as often as they pleased. He also recommended that they should get by heart the most impressive speeches and sentiments from Shakespeare and Roman history.

One of the characteristics of the present superficial

and desultory age is, that parents take so little personal interest in the education of their children. In the upper and middle classes, even where leisure allows, in how few cases is there a parental supervision of the education of families? And yet, who so fit as the parents to undertake this? Of course, the answer to such a proposal, in the majority of cases, would be, that they have not time. It would be useful to inquire what they are doing which is of more importance. Or, probably, they might answer, that they are not able to undertake a systematic training of the intellect and understanding; but, if so, why do they not fit themselves for the task, at least, whilst the children are young? Lord Collingwood made no claims to extraordinary scholarship, more than lies within the reach of persons of almost every class, in the present day. He had no special means of obtaining skill in training. His mind was occupied every moment with the most important affairs, and yet he found time and opportunity for interesting himself in the closest manner in the education of his children. Whatever parents might or might not possess in the way of acquirement, firmness of will and decision of character, the most valuable parts of education, might be enforced and fostered everywhere; and yet, how rarely do we see the least effort made to instil, definitely, the stability of purpose and fixity of conduct and behaviour,

G

which are the chief shield and protection against the
evils of life! It is from the neglect of the elements
of such teaching, that generation after generation,
men and women, remain the sport of circumstance,
the toy of vacillation and indifferency, and the evils
of one generation are repeated in another, without
the least effort being made to stem or uproot them.
Lord Collingwood was wiser. He wished his children
to be able to meet the reverses of life bravely. He
says, "I hope they will be as little torn as possible
by the rude briars that may stretch across their way,
and have spirits firm enough not to mind a little
scratch." He knew how much depended on the
foundation of strong individual energies. He encouraged them by precept, fostered them by training,
and enforced them by example. He never lost sight
of the effort to bestow on his children the anchorage
of firm principle, not to be swayed by the airs of
fashion, the purposeless fluctuations of undiscerning
men and women who are the weathercock of opinion,
the vane to every breath of popular folly which may
sweep within their limited horizon.

Too soon the brief holiday was over. The late
northern spring still lingered; the buds were burst-
ing on the tree; the birds had begun to sing their
madrigals; nature prepared to put on her summer
dress. One short year and the Cerberus of war
began to bark once more. Farewells must be said.

How sad would be the tears of his household at parting with so good a man! Old Scott would come for
a last shake of the hand, no doubt, and his voice
would falter as he said good-bye. But of those
nearer and dearer ones, who shall measure the affliction? Who shall say how blank, how dead, how
silent, the house appeared as he left it, as he turned
for a last, fond, lingering look—yes, imprint it,
Memory, deeply; let it lie graven upon the soul with
all that is imperishable there—a last look at the
place he had called his home, here below, next to the
post of duty! How much bitterer would those tears
have been, how infinitely more sorrowful the parting,
if that could have been foreseen, which a merciful
Heaven had wisely veiled—that this good man, this
tender husband, this thoughtful and affectionate
father, should see the faces of his loved ones no
more.

He remembered this afterwards, when he wrote,

"Since 1793, I have been only one year at home.
To my own children I am scarcely known; but while
I have health and strength to serve my country, I consider that health and strength to be its due; and, if I
serve it successfully, as I have ever done faithfully, my
children will not want for friends."

It was a bitter separation. But to him the sacrifice had been made before; it was only consummated
now.

G 2

Early in May, he embarked in the *Venerable* to join the squadron off Brest. " Here comes Collingwood," said Admiral Cornwallis ; " the last to leave me and the first to rejoin me."

Collingwood now commenced a very arduous duty. Once more he was placed on the blockade service off the coast of Spain. He writes to his father-in-law off Brest, August 9, 1803 :—

"I am lying off the entrance of Brest Harbour, to watch the motions of the French fleet. Our information respecting them is very vague, but we know they have four or five and twenty great ships, which makes it necessary to be alert, and keep our eyes open at all times. I therefore bid adieu to snug beds and comfortable naps at night, never lying down but in my clothes. Sarah's account of our improved house pleases me very much. I hope she will make it as comfortable as possible, and enjoy peace and happiness there, whatever may happen in the world abroad. It will cost a good deal of money, but I have provided for it, as I reckon the comforts of my wife among my chief luxuries ; it is, indeed, the only one which my present situation will allow me to gratify. We hear no news here, and cannot be in more complete seclusion from the world, with only one object in view—that of preventing the French from doing harm."

Many a night did he spend with his trusty lieutenant Clavell, on the quarter-deck, in all sorts of weather, vigilantly watching for the enemy's ships. Often they would lie on deck, or on the carriage of a gun from dusk to dawn, rising from time to time to sweep the dim horizon with their glasses. Sometimes Clavell would remonstrate with his captain upon his unrelaxing toil, but he would simply try to persuade his faithful officer to retire himself, and leave him to watch alone.

An examination of the ship which Collingwood commanded at this time, showed that she was entirely rotten and unseaworthy, and that he and his ship's company had been sailing for six months, only protected from destruction by the thickness of a sheet of copper. Resuming his station on the *Culloden*, Collingwood was promoted Vice-Admiral of the Blue in April 1804.

In the meantime the political horizon had thickened. Napoleon held all Europe in check. His policy was, by long courses of inaction, to wear out the patience and purses of his adversaries, and then to take advantage of any withdrawal of forces. England was the only country which made any decisive stand against his usurpations, and it was to England the nations looked for re-establishment and safety. At first discredited, it was finally evident that all his plans were directed to a meditated invasion of England. For this his whole fleet and forces were reserved, whilst he strove by every means in his power to distract England from his real purpose. He menaced Egypt and India. He endeavoured to

draw the English ships to the West Indies. Nelson
was induced to follow his fleet twice across the
Atlantic; and once, whilst Nelson was on his way to
Egypt on false information, the French ships escaped
out of the Mediterranean by the Straits of Gibraltar.
Seeking thus to divert the English commanders from
his ulterior object, the purpose of Buonaparte was to
prepare a vast army with transports at Boulogne,
which, indeed, had in a great measure been done, to
be rejoined by the French and Spanish fleets whenever the channel should be free, and descent made
upon the English coast. Eighteen thousand men
were to have been landed in Ireland, to be reinforced
by twenty-seven thousand from seven Dutch sail of
the line. "Only let us command the sea three days in
front of Boulogne," said Napoleon to his naval commander-in-chief, Villeneuve, "and we will embark
one hundred and sixty thousand men on two thousand
vessels: six hours master of the channel and we are
masters of the world." He thought Collingwood had
been deceived by his stratagems, and had gone to
India. But let us see where the watchful eyes were
directed, and what the thoughtful brain was planning.
Without any actual knowledge of the circumstances
stated above, as they became known afterwards, but
only directed by his own sagacity, Collingwood
addresses the following letter to Nelson. It is dated
July 21st, 1805 :—

"We approached, my dear lord, with caution, not
knowing whether we were to expect you or the Frenchmen first. I have always had an idea that Ireland alone
was the object they have in view, and still believe that
to be their ultimate destination. They will now liberate
the Ferrol squadron from Calder, make the round of the
bay, and taking the Rochefort people with them, appear
off Ushant, perhaps with thirty-four sail, there to be
joined by twenty more. This appears a probable plan:
for unless it be to bring their powerful fleets and armies
to some great point of service—some rash attempt at
conquest—they have only been subjecting them to
chance of loss, which I do not believe the Corsican
would do without the hope of an adequate reward. The
French Government never aim at little things while
great objects are in view. I have considered the invasion of Ireland as the real mark and butt of all their
operations. Their flight to the West Indies was to take
off the naval force, which proved the great impediment to their undertaking. This summer is big with
events: we may all perhaps have an active share in
them; and I sincerely wish your lordship strength of
body to go through it, and to all others your strength
of mind."

So accurate were these anticipations, and so fully
verified in the issue, that one would almost suppose
them to have been a draught of the instructions
given by Napoleon to Villeneuve, which were subsequently published. With such sharpened foresight
as this in her commanders, England had not much
to fear. She had committed her safety to men who

knew how to look after the trust.   With such heroic
hearts and brave natures to defend her, she could not
fall, for they did not know when they were beaten.
They set odds at defiance and in death were victorious.
What Englishman's heart does not thrill to read
such grand calm words as these; not the mere
ebullitions of animal excitement, but the cool de-
liberations of a purposed resolve : few words, but
pertinent, and only waiting the occasion to be trans-
muted into still stronger deeds?   They are written
to Mr. Blackett, off Cadiz, August 9th, 1805.

" I have just time to tell you that I am as well as can
be, and in great expectation that we shall have a rattling
day of it very soon.   The Spaniards are completely
ready here; they have four thousand troops embarked :
at Carthagena they have many more, and a strong
squadron.   Whenever they come, Sir R. Bickerton is to
join me with his ships, and then there will be two to
one; but we must beat them, or never come home; and
yet I intend it fully.   A dull superiority creates languor;
it is a state like this that rouses the spirits, and makes
us feel as if the welfare of England depended on us
alone.   You shall not be disappointed."

In May 1805, Collingwood took up a station off
Cadiz for the purpose of watching the combined fleets
in that port and stopping their supplies.   The first
thing he did on his arrival there was to detach two
of his best and fastest sailing ships to the aid of
Nelson, who was in chase of the French, to the West

Indies, knowing at the same time what he might have to contend with from the blockaded fleets. Nothing could be more daring. But Collingwood had calculated contingencies, and knew very well what he was doing. It would be deemed a thing perfectly incredible, if it were not beyond all question, that first three and then four English ships of the line, with a frigate and a bomb-vessel, could blockade a port containing a fleet of the enemy's ships "as thick as a wood" effectually and safely, as Collingwood did for a length of time. For this he got, as he deserved to get, great praise. It was an occasion requiring all the foresight, firmness, watchfulness, and judgment of the most experienced tactician. Collingwood was deficient in none of these qualities, and he was ably seconded by the captains and crews of the little squadron. Once he was placed in a very critical position. Whilst they were cruising one morning— it was on the 20th of August—they were surprised by the appearance of ten or eleven sail of the line of the enemy, of whose vicinity they had not the slightest suspicion. "We were only three poor things, with a frigate and a bomb," says Lord Collingwood, in writing to his wife. All sail was set; but the decks were cleared for action. Presently twenty-five more of the enemy appeared; nineteen of them being despatched in pursuit of the English squadron. The *Dreadnought*, which Collingwood commanded, though

a powerful ship, was a bad sailer, but she was well
manned, and if she could not fly she could fight.
Collingwood used to say that nothing could stand
against three telling broadsides delivered within five
minutes, but so well practised had his gunners been
under his daily superintendence, that they could discharge three well-directed broadsides in three minutes
and a half. He commanded all the men not required
in working the ship to lie down, in order that her
motion might be disturbed as little as possible. He
knew he could depend on the other officers of the
squadron. Keeping under steady sail, he edged on
to the current setting towards the Straits. "I am
determined," he said, "they shall not drive me
through the Straits, unless they go along with me."
Pausing, the enemy shortened sail, upon which the
English ships stood towards them, but presently they
came once more in pursuit. It was Collingwood's
intention to have attracted them to the southward-
bearing stream, and then to have drawn them fighting to Gibraltar Bay. But whether the enemy fore-
saw this design, or for whatever cause, they retired
from the chase, and entering the harbour of Cadiz,
rejoined their companions there. Reinforced by one
more ship at night, Collingwood took up his position
as before, and blockaded the harbour.

Collingwood had not depended entirely upon force
or prowess in maintaining his critical position before

the stronghold of the enemy. He had helped himself by stratagem. Two of his ships nearest the harbour constantly telegraphed the movements of the enemy to the other ships which were stationed some distance in the offing. The signals were again telegraphed by the latter as if to other ships still more distant, beyond sight of the enemy. This delusion was kept up so successfully for some time, that the enemy believed the nearer vessels to be but a detachment of the fleet which lay within call. Collingwood wrote from this station to Mr. Blackett, on the 21st of September, 1805, as follows:—

"As a ship will return to England in a few days, I will not lose the opportunity of writing to you, though I have little hope of an answer, for I never hear from England. Even the Admiralty seem to have abandoned me to my own devices; but I am going on very well, and with God's blessing I hope to continue so. The combined fleet in Cadiz is perfectly complete, I believe, now; for the last of the ships that wanted repair came into the bay yesterday. They have thirty-four sail of the line, and I have enough whenever they choose to try their skill. It would be a happy day that would relieve me from this perpetual cruising, which is really wearing me to a lath. The great difficulty I have, is to keep up the health of the men; and it is a subject that requires an unremitted attention, of which we seldom find any person disposed to take the trouble. We get good beef from the Moors; but to bring it requires a number of ships, which I can ill spare. Two hundred bullocks do not serve us a week, and a transport laden with wine about a month. How we are to keep up our water I do not know.

"How happy should I be, could I but hear from home, and know how my dear girls are going on! Bounce is my only pet now, and he is indeed a good fellow: he sleeps by the side of my cot, whenever I lie in one, until near the time of tacking, and then marches off, to be out of the hearing of the guns, for he is not reconciled to them yet. I am fully determined, if I can get home and manage it properly, to go on shore next spring for the rest of my life; for I am very weary. There is no end to my business: I am at work from morning till even; but I daresay Lord Nelson will be out next month. He told me he should; and then what will become of me I do not know. I should wish to go home; but I must go or stay as the exigencies of the times require. This, with all its labour, is a most unprofitable station; but that is not a consideration of much moment to me. What I look to as the first and great object, is to defeat the projects of this combined fleet, of whom I can get little information; but I watch them narrowly, and if they come out will fight them merrily; for on their discomfiture depends the safety of England, and it shall not fail in my hands if I can help it."

"If you had been forced to quit the vicinity of Cadiz," said Nelson, writing to Collingwood afterwards, "England would not have forgiven you."

The position of the blockaded fleet was now such as to be in serious want of provision. Napoleon had victualled the more northerly ports of Brest, Rochefort and Ferrol, not anticipating the detention of his fleet so far south as Cadiz, to which port it had been driven after the action with Sir Robert Calder, who had intercepted it on its way from the West Indies. When he attempted to meet this circumstance by transshipping the supplies, they were effectually cut off by the blockade. It thus happened that the fleet was compelled to come out of port and face its enemies. This crisis was foreseen by the English commanders. Nelson wrote to Collingwood from the Admiralty, September 7th, 1805 :—

"My dear Coll.: I shall be with you in a very few days, and I hope you will remain second in command. You will change the *Dreadnought* for the *Royal, Sovereign*, which I hope you will like."

Nelson, knowing the value of Collingwood's coolness, thoughtfulness, and sagacity, at once treated him in the most confidential manner; sending him his letters to the Admiralty to read, with a despatch box for exchanges of correspondence, telling him to telegraph upon all occasions, and saying, "We are one, and I hope ever shall be." Still more memorable is the letter Nelson wrote to him on the 9th of October :—

"I send you Captain Blackwood's letter; and as I hope *Weazle* has joined, he will have five frigates and a brig. They surely cannot escape us. I wish we

could get a fine day. I send you my plan of attack, as
far as a man dare venture to guess at the very uncertain position the enemy may be found in : but, my
dear friend, it is to place you perfectly at ease respecting my intentions, and to give full scope to your
judgment for carrying them into effect. We can, my
dear Coll., have no little jealousies : we have only one
great object in view—that of annihilating our enemies,
and getting a glorious peace for our country. No man
has more confidence in another than I have in you ;
and no man will render your services more justice than
your very old friend—NELSON AND BRONTE."

When Collingwood changed his ship, he took with
him his first lieutenant, Clavell, and his signal-
lieutenant. As the enemy had heretofore been
persuaded that they were awaited out of the harbour
by a large fleet, when there was only Collingwood's
little squadron, so now they were made to hold a
contrary opinion under converse circumstances. The
real force of the English fleet was concealed, whilst
the enemy was induced to follow a decoy towards
Gibraltar. Villeneuve, the French commander-in-
chief of the combined fleets, thought he might easily
attack the Mediterranean fleet with thirty-three ships
of the line, eighteen French and fifteen Spanish, and
ventured out accordingly. On the 10th of October
Nelson wrote to Collingwood as follows :

" The enemy's fleet are all but out of the harbour :
perhaps this night, with the northerly wind, they may

come forth. The Admiralty could not do less than call your conduct judicious. Everybody in England admired your adroitness in not being forced unnecessarily into the Straits."

On the 19th Nelson sent an invitation to Collingwood to visit him on his ship; but before an answer had reached the *Victory*, the signal was made that the enemy's fleet was coming out of Cadiz, and they were held in chase immediately.

The memorable engagement off Cape Trafalgar, so honourable to the conduct of the British navy, and so important in its results, was fought on the 21st of October, 1805. It will be only necessary here to speak of that part of it in which Collingwood was directly concerned, though there was not a man in the British fleet who did not do credit to his nationality on that occasion.

A south-west wind was blowing and a rather heavy swell rolling shorewards as the morning of this eventful day broke somewhat gloomily. At this hour Collingwood's attendant entered his cabin, finding his master already up and calmly performing a toilette more careful than usual. "Have you seen the French fleet this morning, Smith?" said the admiral, quietly proceeding with his shaving and other operations. "No, sir," said Smith. "Then look out of that window," was the reply, "and you will see something of them; but you will see a great deal more of them presently." Smith looked at the fleet, but still more at the admiral, who did not exhibit the least flush of excitement or disturbance. Meeting Lieutenant Clavell shortly afterwards walking about in a pair of high-topped boots, he said to him, "You had better put on silk stockings as I have done, for if one should get a shot in the leg, they would be so much more manageable for the surgeon." Collingwood had a good wholesome fear of a lee-shore in the shoal water and drifting currents of this part of the coast, and often warned his officers against it. But they said to each other, "We shall hear nothing of a lee-shore to-day." Collingwood walked the decks, encouraged the men, and said to his officers, "Now, gentlemen, let us do something to-day which the world may talk of hereafter." In changing from the *Dreadnought* to the *Royal Sovereign,* although the admiral had left his practised and well-trained crew behind him, he had now the fastest sailing ship in the line, for her coppers had just been cleaned in England. The enemy's ships were drawn in a line slightly curved outwards. The English advanced in two columns, the weather one commanded by Nelson, and the lee division by Collingwood. The English fleet numbered twenty-seven, and the enemy thirty-three ships of the line, exclusive of frigates and smaller vessels.

The *Royal Sovereign* outsailed all the other vessels,

both of her own and the windward division. She
was signalled to break the line at the twelfth ship,
but when Collingwood saw that this was only a two-
decker, and that the next but one astern was a first-
rate, carrying Admiral Alava's flag, he ventured to
disregard orders so far as to make for that vessel.
Again a signal was made from Nelson's ship. "I
wish Nelson would make no more signals," said
Collingwood; " we all know what we are to do." But
the heart of the brave commander was stirred as he
read the memorable words, " England expects that
every man will do his duty," and they flashed from
ship to ship with a joyous shout that filled the air
on every side. Clavell observed Nelson's ship, the
Victory, setting her studding-sails, and wished to do
the same; but his wary commander bade him wait,
as already they had considerably outsailed the rest
of the fleet. Presently a nod from Collingwood sent
the good ship flying far in advance of all the rest. The
men were all commanded to lie down in silence on
the deck. Then up came the *Fougueux*, which was
astern of the *Santa Anna*, and stood before Collingwood's ship to prevent him from breaking the
line. " Steer straight for the Frenchman," cried
Collingwood to his captain, " and take his bowsprit.'
The Frenchman, however, had not calculated on so
much, nor had yet learned that to an English ship,
well-manned and well-commanded, nothing was an

obstacle. He sheered off and opened fire. But Collingwood knew how to speak and how to be silent. Only a few guns were discharged to cover his ship with smoke as he flew to his quarry.

The *Royal Sovereign* was now about a mile in advance of all the rest of the fleet. " See, how that noble fellow, Collingwood, takes his ship into action !" cried Nelson. " Gentlemen," said Collingwood, " what would Nelson give to be here ?" Then it was that the heart of Villeneuve, the commander-in-chief of the combined fleet, sank within him, as he afterwards confessed; for he then felt that a fleet so led into action could not fail to conquer. A little after noon the *Royal Sovereign,* passing astern of the *Santa Anna,* which, Collingwood says, towered over the English ship like a castle, delivered a double-shotted broadside and a half into her stern, tearing it to pieces, and killing or wounding four hundred men. Then she closed with her till the yards crossed, and the two vessels were interlocked. Upon this the enemy opened her thunders, and such was their weight and force, that at the first discharge the *Royal Sovereign* heeled two streaks out of the water. Studding-sails and halliards now gave way. A sail hanging over the gangway hammocks was receiving much damage, when Collingwood called Clavell to come and help him to fold it up, as " it would be wanted another day." It was accordingly rolled up and placed in a boat.

In about a quarter of an hour, and before any other English ship could be brought into action, Captain Rotherham, whose brave deeds on this occasion were eminently conspicuous, came and grasped the hand of the admiral, and said, "I congratulate you, sir; she is slackening her fire, and must soon strike." To have taken the Spanish admiral unassisted, a single ship amongst a fleet of thirty-three sail of the enemy, would indeed have been a triumph; but this was too much, though nearly accomplished. The *Santa Anna*, though almost silent, kept up a feeble fire at intervals, determined to hold out as long as possible, surrounded as she was by her friends, who now came up to render assistance. Indeed, the English ship was at this moment in a critical situation. Once more the *Fougueux* advanced upon her stern and raked her cruelly, whilst at two cables' length from her in the opposite direction the *San Leandro* played upon her bows, and, not quite so far removed on her starboard bow and quarter, the *San Justo* and *L'Indomptable* kept up a murderous fire. So hot was the engagement that the shots were frequently seen to come in contact between the ships. Thus surrounded, the enemy hoped to destroy the English ship before she could be succoured. But their very eagerness frustrated itself; for they found that they damaged their own vessels by so close a cross fire almost as much as their opponent, and as other ships now began to come up, Collingwood was once more left alone with the *Santa Anna*.

In the meantime the undaunted admiral, who stood upon the poop, seeing the marines fall thickly around him, directed the gallant Captain Vallack to remove his men from that position; although he thought fit to remain there himself some time longer. Whilst there he received some severe wounds and bruises, which, however, he never noticed in his despatches, nor even mentioned to his family until several months afterwards, when in writing to Lady Collingwood, he says,

" Did I not tell you how my leg was hurt? It was by a splinter—a pretty severe blow. I had a good many thumps, one way or the other; one in the back, which I think was the wind of a great shot, for I never saw anything that did it. You know nearly all were killed or wounded on the quarter-deck and poop but myself, my captain, and secretary, Mr. Cosway, who was of more use to me than any officer, after Clavell. The first inquiry of the Spaniards was about my wound, and exceedingly surprised they were when I made light of it; for when the captain of the *Santa Anna* was brought on board, it was bleeding and swelled, and tied up with a handkerchief. Since you have informed me that my despatches are admired, I am exceedingly ambitious of giving you a second edition with improvements."

To follow the narrative: presently he descended

to. the quarter-deck, desiring the men not to fire a single shot in waste. He directed some of the guns himself, encouraging the sailors, particularly commending one of his gunners, a black man, afterwards killed, who, whilst he stood beside him, fired ten times directly into the port-hole of the *Santa Anna.* At one time the *Fougueux* got on the quarter of the *Royal Sovereign* so closely that the quarter-deck carronades were brought to bear on the forecastle so hotly that she withdrew, keeping up a safe fire till the *Mars* and *Belleisle* coming up, drove her away; the latter of which gave a distant broadside into the *Santa Anna* in passing.

For twenty minutes was this perilous position maintained; the *Royal Sovereign* had remained the centre of a battery pouring upon her and into her showers of shot from every side: for twenty minutes—an age under such circumstances—the brave English ship had suffered all the worst that the concentrated force of the enemy could do to her. She had done this before another English vessel could be brought into close action. As the commanders of the rest of Collingwood's line forced their ships forward with every sail set to the assistance of their admiral, they looked with the greatest anxiety to see if his flag yet flew to the wind; but it never fell. As the clouds of smoke cleared away, it still fluttered above the battle, an emblem of the dauntless and unconquerable spirit of the brave commander. So astounded was one of the captains of the division at the promptitude, energy, and gallantry which was displayed by the *Royal Sovereign*, that for some moments he stood bereft of everything but wonder and admiration.

Between a quarter and half-past two, or in a little more than an hour from the first shot, the *Santa Anna*, one side of which was almost entirely blown away, struck to the *Royal Sovereign* at a critical moment; for as she did so the mizzen-mast of the latter came down with a crash, the fore and main-masts being in a condition to follow, which they presently did.

It was about this time, or possibly a little later, that an officer from the *Victory* came to inform Collingwood of Nelson's wound, with an affectionate message from the dying commander. Collingwood looked the man in the face and asked him if the wound was mortal; the officer said he hoped not, but Collingwood read in his eye the fatal tale, and at once divined that he should see his old friend and comrade no more.*

* As this circumstance is stated upon Lord Collingwood's authority alone, Mr. James, in his Naval History, has thought proper to challenge its truth. Lord Collingwood says, in a letter to Mrs. Moutray, "It was about the middle of the action when an officer came from the *Victory*, to tell me he [Nelson] was wounded. He sent his love to me, and desired

Collingwood having shifted his flag to the *Euryalus* in consequence of the dilapidated condition of the *Royal Sovereign*, the latter was taken in tow, and Captain Blackwood, the commander of the *Euryalus*, was sent to convey the Spanish admiral on board; but as he was wounded, and said

---

me to conduct the fleet. I asked the officer if the wound was dangerous, and he by his look told what he could not speak, nor I reflect upon now without suffering again the anguish of that moment."

The request that Collingwood should undertake the command of the fleet certainly appears incongruous with the words of the wounded admiral, who, when Captain Hardy asked him if Collingwood must assume command, replied, "Not whilst I live, Hardy." It would, however, be very presumptuous on this account to deny the truth of Collingwood's statement. The resignation of command may have been intended to be understood prospectively, or it may have been that Nelson, when he sent the message, believed himself at the point of death, but on rallying a little still clung to the post of duty. In any case, the message was a purely formal one, and had no official importance, since Nelson knew perfectly well that his wound was mortal, that he could not long survive it, and that the command must perforce devolve on his coadjutor. Whatever view we may take of the circumstance, it is certain that Collingwood cannot for a moment be suspected of having made a false statement knowingly. It is particularly mentioned in several private letters, in his report to the Admiralty, and in a subsequent account of the battle given to the Duke of Clarence, and always in almost the same terms; and as the statement was immediately published, both the public and those who took part in the engagement being interested in every detail, a misrepresentation of a matter of fact would undoubtedly have been at once detected and contradicted.

to be in a dying condition, his captain came instead. The captain had already yielded his sword in the *Royal Sovereign*. When he came on board that vessel he asked one of the sailors in broken English what it was called. "The *Royal Sovereign*," was the answer. "It should be called the *Royal Devil* rather," said he, laying his hands upon one of the guns. Cheer after cheer rang through the fleet as the enemy's ships surrendered one after another. When Captain Blackwood hastened to the *Victory*, the battle not yet being over, Nelson lay dead in the cockpit. Of Collingwood's crew, forty-seven were killed and ninety-four wounded. The swords of the first and second officers of the *Santa Anna* were surrendered. One of these was said or supposed to be that of the admiral, Alava, who, as has been stated, was reported to be mortally wounded in the cabin. He was carried into Cadiz when his vessel found her way into that port, and recovering from his wound, thenceforward claimed his liberty and an untarnished honour; a circumstance which justly provoked the contempt and indignation of the honourable and upright English commander.

The future conduct of the day, with the head command of the fleet, devolved upon Admiral Collingwood, than whom there was none fitter. But what a fleet! Most of the ships were totally incapacitated for sailing, and many seriously damaged in the hull. In this condition, with a dead wind shoreward and seventeen prizes in charge, after riding out the gale three or four hours, the fleet was called to anchor. This, however, was found to be impossible; few ships having anchor or cable in a serviceable condition. But when night came the wind veered and the ships drifted out seawards.

The same day Collingwood transmitted his thanks and acknowledgments to every man and officer in the fleet, saying, "Every individual appeared a hero on whom the glory of his country depended." The next day he issued an order for a general thanksgiving as follows:—

"The Almighty God, whose arm is strength, having of His great mercy been pleased to crown the exertions of His Majesty's fleet with success, in giving them a complete victory over their enemies on the twenty-first of this month; and that all praise and thanksgiving may be offered up to the Throne of Grace for the great benefit to our country, and to mankind, I have thought proper that a day should be appointed of general humiliation before God, and thanksgiving for His merciful goodness, imploring forgiveness of sins, a continuation of His divine mercy, and His constant aid to us in defence of our country's liberties and laws, without which the utmost efforts of man are nought. I direct, therefore, that —— be appointed for this holy purpose."

Very strong gales blowing after the battle, it was

found necessary to remove the crews of some of the captured vessels and to scuttle them, lest they should drift back into their own port. This was a sad blow to Collingwood. Captain Blackwood, in a letter to his wife written at this time, says, "Could you witness the grief and anxiety of Admiral Collingwood (who has done all that an admiral could do) you would be very deeply affected." Admiral Villeneuve, the French commander-in-chief, was taken into the *Euryalus*. All the wounded of the enemy were treated with the utmost kindness and consideration; some of them being sent on shore to receive the benefit of their own hospitals, without even the agreement of terms of exchange, only a receipt for the number being given. The generosity of this conduct was not only acknowledged, but reciprocated by the Spaniards with every mark of enthusiastic gratitude. Two days after the battle the combined fleet collected a remnant of ten sail, with the intention of attacking the English ships, but on preparations being made to oppose them, they desisted. Admiral Collingwood stated afterwards that, besides the hope of another engagement with the remnant of the enemy's fleet, another reason for his keeping the sea at this time (which he said, "had a little pride in it") was to show the enemy that it "was not a battle nor a storm which could remove a British squadron from the station they were directed to hold."

It was a glorious but dear-bought victory. "In three hours," says Collingwood, "the combined forces were annihilated, upon their own shores, at the entrance of their port, amongst their own rocks." Nineteen sail of the enemy surrendered to the English flag, four admirals were taken, and about twenty thousand prisoners, including troops, besides killed and wounded. The ruin of the enemy's fleet was complete: the designs of Napoleon, as far as sea-service went, were at once and for ever crushed.

Not least noteworthy in the conduct of Admiral Collingwood on this occasion was the modesty with which his own part in this memorable engagement was referred to in his official despatch, a circumstance remarked with much admiration by naval historians and biographers. He says in this document: " The commander-in-chief in the *Victory* led the weather column, and the *Royal Sovereign*, which bore my flag, the lee. The action began at twelve o'clock, by the leading ships of the columns breaking through the enemy's line :"—and that is every word he says about himself or his doings as far as the fight was concerned. What noble reticence! What a lesson for the boaster; the newspaper hero! How characteristic of the fine nature of the man! What a ring of the true metal is there in it! Such men as this are the bulwarks of a state and the safeguard of a nation: <u>for their words are few, and their deeds are</u> <u>great and they do not count them.</u>

In the same despatch all the feelings of the man reveal themselves through the formality of official prescription. " I have not only," he says, " to lament, in common with the British navy and the British nation, in the fall of the commander-in-chief, the loss of a hero, whose name will be immortal, and his memory ever dear to his country: but my heart is rent with the most poignant grief for the death of a friend, to whom by many years of intimacy, and a perfect knowledge of the virtues of his mind, which inspired ideas superior to the common race of men, I was bound by the strongest ties of affection—a grief to which even the glorious occasion in which he fell does not bring the consolation which, perhaps, it ought." His regrets for the loss of Nelson were deep and bitter. " Oh, had Nelson lived," he writes to Lord Radstock, " how complete had been my happiness, how perfect my joy! Now, whatever I have felt like pleasure has been so mixed with the bitterness of woe, that I cannot exult in our success as it would be pardonable to do." Again, in writing to Mrs. Moutray, he says, " You, my dear madam, who know what our friendship was, can judge what I have felt. All the praise and acclamations of joy for our victory only bring to my mind what it has cost."

Lord Collingwood's letter to the Admiralty on the

subject of promotions was expressed in very generous terms. His own commission, by which he was vested with full power as a commander-in-chief, was sent to him with the expression of every confidence in his judgment and skill. That this was well bestowed was confirmed by the circumstance that the instructions forwarded with it as to the conduct of the fleet had already been anticipated and carried out. From the King, the Duke of Clarence, and from both houses of parliament eventually, Collingwood received the most ample acknowledgments. He was raised to the peerage under the title of Baron Collingwood of Caldburne and Hethpoole. He received the thanks and freedom of most of the cities in Great Britain. A pension of two thousand pounds a year was conferred upon him during his lifetime, and in the event of his death, one thousand pounds a year to Lady Collingwood, and five hundred pounds a year to each of his daughters. It appears there had been some difficulty at first in finding where Collingwood's estate lay, in order to furnish his title. "I thought," said he, "that all the world knew I was no landlord."

The way in which he supported his honours is something very delightful to contemplate. We find him writing to Lady Collingwood, on the 6th of December, as follows:

"It would be hard if I could not find one hour to

write a letter to my dearest Sarah, to congratulate her
on the high rank to which she has been advanced by
my success. Blessed may you be, my dearest love, and
may you long live the happy wife of your happy
husband! I do not know how you bear your honours,
but I have so much business on my hands, from dawn
to midnight, that I have hardly time to think of mine,
except it be in gratitude to my king, who has so
graciously conferred them upon me. But there are so
many things of which I might justly be a little proud
—for extreme pride is folly—that I must share my
gratification with you. . . . . A week before the war,
at Morpeth, I dreamed, distinctly, many of the circumstances of our late battle off the enemy's port, and I
believe I told you of it at the time : but I never dreamed
that I was to be a peer of the realm. How are my
darlings? I hope they will take pains to make themselves wise and good, and fit for the station to which
they are raised."

Again he writes, ten days later :

"I write merely to say that I am well, and as busy as
any creature can be. How I shall ever get through all
the letters which are written to me, I know not. I
labour from dawn till midnight till I can hardly see ;
and, as my hearing fails me too, you will have but a
mass of infirmities in your poor lord, whenever he
returns to you. I suppose I must not be seen to work
in my garden now ; but tell old Scott that he need not
be unhappy on that account. Though we shall never
again be able to plant the ' Nelson ' potatoes, we will
have them of some other sort, and right noble cabbages
to boot, in great perfection. You see I am styled of

Hethpoole and Caldburne. Was that by your direction? I should prefer it to any other title if it was; and I rejoice, my love, that we are an instance that there are other and better sources of nobility than wealth."

Collingwood was proud at this time to hear that the King had written to the Admiralty, saying that the more he heard of the proceedings of the fleet under Collingwood's command, the more he was pleased with its management. An evidence of the esteem and affection with which Collingwood was regarded by the officers in the service, is furnished by the circumstance that many of the captains expressed the desire that he would give them a general notice whenever he should go to court, and they would travel five hundred miles, if necessary, in order to attend him.

At the beginning of 1806, he writes to Mr. Blackett:—

" I hardly know how we shall be able to support the dignity to which his Majesty has been pleased to raise me. Let others plead for pensions; I can be rich without money, by endeavouring to be superior to everything poor. I would have my services to my country unstained by any interested motive; and old Scott and I can go on in our cabbage garden, without much greater expense than formerly."

On his elevation to the peerage, as Lord Collingwood had no sons, he asked, as a favour, that his title might be continued through his elder daughter, in order, as he said, that "future Collingwoods might manifest, in future ages, their fidelity to their country." It was the only request he ever made of his country, the only favour he ever asked for himself. One would have thought that, under the circumstances, taking his long absence from home into consideration, his meritorious services, his self-immolation to the benefit of his country, that no reasonable request would have been denied to him, however unexampled by precedent. But from that elevated point of view and disregard of small things, excepting when they are marks of official importance, which sometimes characterise the function of states-manship, it was thought fit to put the question by with the usual conventional phrases. Though the request was repeated, it was never granted, and Collingwood lived to look upon such a desire with the utmost in-difference. For, indeed, what were all these things? What was the best that a great nation could do for him? Could these repay him for long years of in-difference, neglect, the toilsome, conscientious service, the hardship, the suffering, the self-sacrifice? All these had accompanied him through a lifetime. His country had delayed to recognise them as long as it could. It had withheld from him the meed of his lofty conduct and grand interpretation of the duties of his function, until, out of very shame, it could withhold it no longer. He was made no greater by success of arms, for he had all along been doing his duty to his country in far more difficult ways than the fighting of battles. His whole life had been a battle. He had laid down everything for his country; home, personal tastes and feelings, the tranquillities of retirement, the social and domestic pleasures he was so well fitted to enjoy. All these he had given away; what gold, what honours could repay him the gift? No, it was not these which constituted his reward; it was not these which could compensate him for his self-sacrifice; it was not the hard-won and tardily acknowledged gratitude and appreciation of his country, which could be a satisfactory reward for sacrifices so great: public honours, he very well knew, were given or withheld at pleasure, were almost as often bestowed on an unworthy as on a worthy object. He had something better than these, which lifted his soul far above them. It was the consciousness that he had really deserved them; it was the feeling that he had done his duty; it was the sense of an accomplished destiny. He could look back over a life which had been always led by the loadstar of conscientious rectitude. He had always fought under the banner inscribed with the legend, " True to myself, to my country, and to my fellow men." He found no dark spot in the whole region of memory, which reproached him with heartless, selfish, or time-serving conduct. It was all open as

I

day. Neither was he honest from policy. He loved honesty better than policy, and it did not shame him. He had—what seems so little to be generally the case now—a perfect faith in honesty, truth, uprightness, and rectitude. He valued them in and for themselves alone. His nobility of soul was not the offspring of self-interest, it was not imposed by external law; it was the wholesome life-breath which nourished his being and sustained his entire course of action; it gave vitality, force, and energy to the dry bones of prescription ; it lighted the dreary roads of a monotonous and wearisome service with the persistent radiance of a beacon : it was the necessary element, and essential condition of his existence. Truly, he had found the right riches.

Even for the poor honours awarded to him he had to pay in more ways than one. He writes to Lady Collingwood :

"My bankers tell me that all my money in their hands is exhausted by fees on the peerage, and that I am in their debt, which is a new epoch in my life, for it is the first time I was ever in debt since I was a midshipman. Here I get nothing; but then my expenses are nothing, and I do not want it, particularly now that I have got my knives, forks, teapot, and the things you were so kind as to send me."

But it was not only in money that he payed for his justly-won honours. Writing at another time to Lady Collingwood, he says :

"I am not pleased at what occurred in Parliament about my pension, or that my family should have been represented as one whose existence depended on a gift of money; and I have told Lord Castlereagh my mind upon this subject.   Though I do not consider poverty to be criminal, yet nobody likes to be held up as an object of compassion.   Poor as we are, we are independent.   To possess riches is not the object of my ambition, but to deserve them: but I was in hope I should have got another medal; of that, indeed, I was ambitious.   The report that medals are not to be given is a great disappointment to the fleet: but perhaps it is right.   Sometimes they were obtained too easily, and seemed to put all upon a footing, when the degrees of merit were very unequal."

The question of money, however, was shortly afterwards set at rest.   Lord Collingwood's cousin, Mr. Edward Collingwood, of Dissington, died, and left him some property and valuable estates.   A congratulation which he received on this event from the Spanish Marquis de la Solana, who had heard of the circumstance, sent under flag of truce from Cadiz, is interesting for its kindliness and good nature, and as showing the esteem in which Collingwood was held:

"This act of justice and generosity," he says, "is the effect of the enthusiasm which your Excellency's character inspired in the deceased, and does honour to his memory.   Permit me, while sympathising with your Excellency in the feelings which the loss of a

good friend must have excited, to rejoice at your
increase of fortune, which I am sure your Excellency
will use with the same greatness of soul which
distinguishes all the rest of your actions."

It is pleasant to find a little mark of Lord
Collingwood's thoughtfulness on this occasion in
commending the dog of his deceased relative to the
particular care of Lady Collingwood. " I need not
tell you, my dear," he says, " to be very kind to Mr.
Collingwood's dog; for I am sure you will, and so
will I, whenever I come home."

In spite of his advance in rank, Lord Collingwood
was for a long time destitute of the simplest con-
veniences of living. His soup was served in a tin
pan, and he was obliged to borrow a pewter teapot
for his breakfast. He says, " I have had a great
destruction of my furniture and stock; I have
hardly a chair that has not a shot in it, and many
have lost both legs and arms without hope of pension.
My wine broke in moving and my pigs were slain in
battle; and these are heavy losses where they
cannot be replaced."   Indeed, he was no stranger to
personal privation of the most necessary articles at
various periods during the service. In the middle of
June 1808, we find him writing to Lady Collingwood, off Cadiz, " I am a poor lack-linen swain, with
nothing but a few soldiers' shirts, which I got at
Gibraltar. All my own were left at Malta and

Palermo, and when I shall get them I know not; but such wants give me little disquietude."

Lord Collingwood at this time had many annoyances. The ministers had withheld their vote of thanks as long as possible from the noble defenders of their country, and had only corresponded with him once in three months. "Everybody," says Collingwood, "seems to rejoice more than the ministers." He was anxious on the subject of promotions, and upon some of the most deserving of these, ventured upon his own account, he received a sharp letter from Lord Barham, the first Lord of the Admiralty, reserving to that body the right of promotion, excepting in the case of vacancies caused by death or resulting from a court-martial. The truth was, that Collingwood, by appointing able and deserving officers to advanced posts in the fleet, was infringing on the privileges of those idlers and danglers who were ever at the elbow of place-hunters and time servers; and to these the care of human life, valuable ships, and national honour were committed. "I see the names of some very indifferent young men in the promotion," says Collingwood, in a letter to Lord Radstock, "who never go to sea without meeting some mischief, for want of common knowledge and care. Every three brigs that come here, commanded by three boys, require a dock-yard. The ships of the line never have anything for artificers to do. I have sent some home, because they could not be maintained in this country, and their service amounted to nothing. Better to give them pensions and let them stay on shore."

Lord Collingwood now entered on a new phase of his career. His duties became almost altogether diplomatic. In the national tempests which devastated Europe, of which Buonaparte was the first mover, which seemed to turn every man's hand against his brother, in the endless political complications, locked and interlocked, extending themselves even to the Eastern quarter of the globe, the fine tact, judgment, and skilful powers of negotiation possessed by Lord Collingwood were indispensable: they found no substitute. As, however, my object here is not to give an historical narrative of the political situation of these times, or even, as I have already said, to furnish a circumstantial biography of Collingwood, but to present, as far as I am able, a fair delineation of his character and its moral significances, I shall not attempt to lay before the reader any account of the perplexing occasions on which he was henceforward called to act, referring him to more special biographies or histories for a particular account of them.

The difficulties of Lord Collingwood's service were from this time very great. His labours were incessant.

His correspondence increased very largely. He writes to Mr. Blackett on the 6th of March, 1806: "I have a most arduous time of it, and affairs are growing so critical all around me, that I scarce know which to take up first. The business of the fleet appears trifling and easy when compared with the many important things I have to settle." He still held the station off Cadiz amidst many disadvantages. He had sixteen sail of the line, some of which had suffered much in the last engagement. A squadron of twenty sail of the enemy was expected at Cadiz with the intention of entering the Mediterranean, which Collingwood was anxious to prevent. A circumstance which made his duties still more onerous was that the Admiralty threw upon him the full responsibility of doing everything; as he found it impossible to get directions from them. "The Admiralty have abandoned me," he says; "I never hear from them, but am labouring for everything that is to promote the interest of my country." In vain he asked for directions, for more ships, for promotions of the most deserving officers. The oracle was quite dumb. Day after day passed, and the whole machinery of the fleet stood still, as far as the Admiralty were concerned, although the occasion was most pressing, through the supineness of the official drones who held the keys of the state and the reins of the affairs of the nation.

Perhaps amongst the greatest trials to energy and conscientiousness in the discharge of duty should be numbered those resulting from the indifference and inaction of others on whom they are in a great measure forced to depend for their free exercise— incumbrances which lie like the boulders dropped by old-world icebergs in the middle of fertile vales; of no use in themselves, and only forming obstacles to cultivation and progress, or like a broken shaft or disjointed crank in an otherwise serviceable piece of machinery, they paralyze every other part, though in itself in perfect working order. But, indeed, these statesman-like dawdlers were not content with the negative mischief of leaving things alone; they were, as has been already stated, actively doing what they could to sap the life out of the navy by appointing persons to situations which they were totally unfitted to fill. Promotions were given in exchange for votes in parliament, for which, of course, nobody took the trouble to fit himself, seeing they could be had without merit or ability. At the time Collingwood was complaining of the want of efficient officers in the fleet, there were nearly three thousand lieutenants on the navy-list, of whom not more than two thousand were actively employed. Collingwood, Nelson, and the Duke of Wellington were all of opinion that promotions ought to be rapid, timed to the occasion, and be bestowed directly by the commander-in-chief.   But such a mode of procedure did not suit the purposes of the political jugglers at home.   Many experienced officers either retired in disgust at seeing incompetent boys promoted over their heads, or else begged, almost heart and spirit-broken, for employment, begging in vain.   In March 1806, Collingwood writes to Mr. Blackett: .

"Nothing can have been more neglectful than the Admiralty have been.   I have not made an officer, except in the death vacancies; nor, indeed, have they written a letter to me these three months, except one short one, desiring me to account for all my prisoners. They ought to be content, for I defy any person to devote himself more to the service than I do, for I spare neither body nor mind."

In vain Collingwood sought to advance his able and active lieutenant, Clavell, who was only finally appointed to the rank of post-captain on a death vacancy, with which the direction at home had nothing to do.   To show the indifferent treatment which Collingwood received at the hands of the Admiralty, and the firmness with which he could speak on such an occasion, a letter may be quoted, addressed to Lord Barham on the 28th of March, 1806 :

"On the subject of the appointments, I hope your lordship will excuse my expressing my great disappointment that the only officer for whom I was

particularly anxious, or whom I recommended to your
lordship to be promoted, has been passed over unnoticed ;
and I can now say, what will scarcely be credited, and
what I am willing to believe your lordship is not aware
of, that I am the only commander in that fleet who has
not had, by the courtesy of the Admiralty, an opportunity
to advance one officer of any description.   The misfortune I had in losing two friends in Captains Duff and
Cooke, made it necessary that I should fill their places,
which I did, as justice demanded, by promoting the
first lieutenants of the *Victory* and *Royal Sovereign*.
My first lieutenant stands where I placed him, in the
Weazle, covered with his wounds, while some of those
serving in private ships are post-captains.   Lieutenant
Landless, the only person I recommended to your lordship, is an old and a valuable officer ; he has followed
me from ship to ship all the war.   A complaint which
he had in his eyes prevented his going into the *Sovereign*
when I removed a few days before the action ; but I did
hope that my earnest recommendation to your lordship
might have gained him favour.   My other lieutenant,
who removed with me into the *Sovereign*, was killed in
the action, and thereby saved from the mortification to
which, otherwise, he would probably have been subjected.   The junior lieutenants who came out in the
Sovereign were gentlemen totally unknown to me ; and
as I do not know their names, I cannot tell whether
they are advanced or not.   The commissions sent out to
me for midshipmen of that ship I have returned to the
Admiralty, as she is in England.

    " I cannot help thinking that there must have been
something in my conduct of which your lordship did

not approve, and that you have marked your disapprobation by thus denying to my dependents and friends
what was given so liberally to other ships of the fleet;
for I have heard that the *Defence* and *Defiance* had each
of them two lieutenants promoted on the recommendation of their captains. If there was anything incorrect
in me, of which your lordship disapproved, I am truly
sorry for it; but I am not conscious of what nature it can
be, for my days and nights have been devoted to the
service."

He says in another place that, " few line-of-battle
ships have more than two or three officers who are
seamen; the rest are boys, fine children in their
mothers' eyes, and the facility with which they get
promoted makes them indifferent as to their qualifications."   Very sound were his opinions on the
subject of advancement.   He says, " When one
considers that in all great bodies of men who are in
any profession, a large proportion of them engage in
it more from motives of individual interest than from
public spirit, all laws, rules, and regulations should
have this principle in view, and the interests of those
who really serve should be advanced."

To a mind so sensitive to justice and the claims of
desert as was Lord Collingwood's, these abuses of
power, the neglect of merit, and disregard of the
courses of business by those whom England had
placed in the office of the ministry were galling
beyond measure. A nature without the safeguard of

a more assured support would undoubtedly have been crushed by them. But the casual and uncertain opinions and conduct of others were not Collingwood's chief or only dependencies. He had a more stable kingdom in which to take refuge. He knew what it was to hold the thorny road of power conscientiously, and did not expect it to be strewn with roses. He had drunk of the robust draught which gave him heart against a sea of troubles. It was a tonic of the most astringent nature. It steeled him against neglect, indifference, supineness, and injustice; and he triumphed over them. They might baffle and worry him, but they could not penetrate his armour. He held an impregnable tenure which was quite out of their reach. He had a standard and a code which they could not impeach or disturb. It was his function to go through a straightforward course; to hold his way unflinchingly, not deviating either to the right hand or the left. He could not command or control the actions of others, he could not frame the world after his own model; but one thing he could and did do: he could say, Here I take my stand upon the foundations of rectitude, and I will not be removed, though the world itself shake beneath my feet; no, not if it should fall in ruins around me. He could hold his head up above the tempestuous flood of fallacious human interests, and whilst he saw the great mass of mankind driven hither and thither by every wind and wave, vaguely drifting to and fro, he could cast himself with full confidence on the bosom of the storm, and breast its billows with a brave heart, strong in the confidence that he should reach the shore supported by the indestructible stays of a life whose bases were firmly fixed in the stabilities of Truth and Duty.

Besides the unfailing refuge of all honest and upright minds, Collingwood had still another source of hope and consolation, quite untouched by the maladministrations and iniquitous truckling which went on around him. He had a quiet bower of rest, dim with the soft green foliage of his northern home. He had the memory of wife and child, more dear to him than his own life, the thought of whom would come gushing up when the pulse of energy beat slowly, and the overtaxed brain collapsed with weariness. Visions of delightful hours would come to him —of long summer days, of pleasant toil enlivened by the voices and presence of those he held dearest on earth. His daughters would repay all his care bestowed on their education and training, and greet him once more with the welcome name of " father." They would embody and exemplify the great principles of his life. He would see in them the personification of his best desires, the fruits of his most earnest struggles. Here he would find a justly earned rest, the crown of his toil, in a peaceful retirement, free from the world's pageantry, its bustling frivolities, its false standards, vapid amusements, and sickening assumptions.

"Bless me," said he, once, after indulging in the delightful dream of a week at home, "what a joy! I am giddy at the thought."

In the midst of the desert of turmoil and distraction by which he was now surrounded, it is pleasant to light upon a little oasis of unbroken joy, a diamond drop of pure delight, a crystal rill from a living fountain. I scarcely know anything more touching in the history of the human heart than these few words, coming from such a man at such a time. They are addressed to his daughters :

"My darlings, little Sarah and Mary :—I was delighted with your last letters, my blessings, and desire you to write to me very often, and tell me all the news of the city of Newcastle and town of Morpeth. I hope we shall have many happy days, and many a good laugh together yet. Be kind to old Scott; and when you see him weeding my oaks, give the old man a shilling. May God Almighty bless you !"

On the 10th of March, in this year (1806), Lord Collingwood writes a very characteristic letter to Mrs. Moutray.

"I am feeling exceedingly interested," he says, "just now for our dear Kate; her happy establishment with health and comfort, and all sorts of blessings around her, would give me great pleasure. Mr. De Lacy's establishment in the world as to rank is most respectable, his fortune enough for comfort, which is so superior to grandeur, that though I wish her in my heart everything good, I hardly wish her richer. Besides, it is pleasing to have something in prospect; it keeps hope awake. I have been poor enough; but of all the things I ever wished for, money was never one. Contentment makes wealth. I have fattened upon that, and never was there a happier house than mine, when I am at home. Besides, we see so many rich creatures whose wealth only makes them more conspicuously contemptible, that I am sure it has nothing to do with happiness.

" But while I am railing at riches, I hear I am made very rich. For every mark of the approbation of my King and country, I am truly grateful; but a pension is one of the last things I should have thought of asking for. The King gave me a signal proof of his approbation by ennobling me, and by those two letters which he directed to be written of me to the Admiralty, which to me are still more than patents of nobility. The general applause of the country has made me rich indeed in what is most valuable to me. These things have filled my head, not with vanity, or pride, or conscious superiority—no, indeed, the very reverse. It is racked to find means of proving further that I am not unworthy of these high distinctions."

Not less interesting is a letter written to Lady Collingwood, some months afterwards, in which we observe the same disregard for false standards, the same indifference to wealth, contempt for its abuse, and disapproval of making either the getting or spending of it one of the principal objects of life; neither must its pure strain of high, manly affection be overlooked.

"I rejoiced to hear that you and all my family were well. I could have been very, very happy indeed to have been with you; but when is that blessed day to come? I received a letter from ——, to thank me for the presents I had sent, and I must thank you most heartily for having anticipated me in that which I would gladly have done myself if I had been there. Oh, my Sarah, how I admire in you that kindness of heart and gene- rosity that delights to give pleasure to those you love! You will, you do understand me, that if ever I mention the word economy, it is that you should always be enabled to do a kind and handsome thing when the occasion arises; and none know how to do so better than you. I shall never have length of life enough to tell you how I love in you those virtues that are every day my admiration. With respect to that matter in which we and —— are jointly interested, I cannot but wonder at their unreasonableness in requiring 600*l.* per annum for that which we have hitherto been content to let for 80*l.*; but they will outwit themselves, for I would not, for all the collieries in Northumberland, be a party to such an extortion. A fair increase of rent is allowable, but this demand is beyond all bounds. I have written enough about money; and between ourselves, Sarah, I believe there is more plague in it than comfort, and that the limits of our Morpeth garden and the lawn would have afforded us as much happiness as we shall ever have. I have lived long enough in the world to know that human happiness has nothing to do with exteriors ; then let us cultivate it in our minds. The parliamentary grant is, I own, lessened in my estimation, when it is only shared by those who laboured in common with those who did nothing. The honour of the thing is lost, and it only becomes a mere matter of money. But they have used us shabbily about that whole business ; for the poor seamen who fought a battle that set all England in an uproar, and all the poets and painters at work, have not at this moment received one sixpence of prize-money. I mean those who are here ; for I do not know what they have done for them in England, as I never hear anything about it."

How honourable are such sentiments as these, both to the head and heart of the brave commander ! With what a simplicity of assurance does he let his wife into the secret that, " there is more plague than comfort in money," as caviare to the multitude, as a fact not likely to be appreciated by the world at large, or even understood by it—indeed, likely to be looked upon as something absolutely ridiculous, altogether too foolish ! And yet, what a sterling truth is there at the bottom of it ! Riches and fame, especially the former, are, we all know, popularly regarded as synonymous with happiness ; as ends, in themselves, perfectly satisfactory and sufficient in the realisation. Yet what a mistake lies in such an

K

opinion! A man shall get up early and go to bed late, and spend himself labouring earnestly to accumulate wealth, which he has been taught to consider as the means of purchasing happiness; but he has no sooner acquired it, than, lo! the delusion vanishes. Where are the roses and soft delights which were to be as an anodyne to his soul? Where are the glory and the light which should make life beautiful? Where is the magic touch, which, by a stroke of its golden wand, can change the dull dross of existence to the perfect workmanship of the soul's brightest ideal? Where is this Eldorado, this land of bliss, wherein Time and Joy, linked hand in hand, festoon the sunny hours, and dance their airy round untouched by pain or sorrow? It has vanished, vanished just at the moment of his grasping it; as far out of reach as ever. His wealth is there, but he does not know how to convert it into that happiness of which it was supposed to be the equivalent. He cannot translate it into the unknown quantity. He goes to Rome and Naples, but the real, spiritual land of peace and beauty is closed against him, he does not reach that. The eyes—the soul's eyes—do not see aright, the chords do not vibrate, the lyre is unstrung and out of tune. He roofs himself with a house of a hundred chambers, but he finds he can only use one; he spreads his table with delicacies, but appetite fails; he surrounds himself with attendants and entrenches himself in society; human passions come into play, distraction ensues. He begins to ask himself how much enjoyment he gets out of life more than the man of moderate means. He asks himself if any of the purchases which wealth can make, beyond a fulfilment of the simpler wants of life, bodily and mental, are at all adequate to its accredited importance, or if they compensate for any care bestowed upon them at the expense of the higher life, character, conduct, and culture. Then the dream begins to dissipate, and he learns, gradually and slowly, but very conclusively, at last, that the art of riches is not in acquiring more than necessity and prudence demand, but in using well that which we have; that, indeed, happiness does not lie in *getting* or in *having* anything, but in *being* something. He finds that the faculty of happiness resides in the inner kingdom— is not to be had from without; that it is to be cultivated by spiritual instruments—the lofty philosophy which disdains the paltry byways of life; the nobility of mind which looks continually to the highest; the fostering thought which nourishes the life and being of a beautiful soul unstained by selfishness and meanness, seeking to raise itself towards the perfect structure, by one crystal stone—one noble deed or elevating thought—placed upon another, until its starry domes and glistening pinnacles kiss the sun and gladden the face of day.

But this is an old-fashioned philosophy or religion ; It has no high ritual; it has no sounding title; it does not appeal to the emotions ; it does not invite either dispute or controversy; it affords no material for scholastic acumen or academic display ; there is no food in it for an ecclesiastical law-court ; there is nothing in its acceptance which could produce a remonstrance or protest from a bishop, or call forth a correspondence in the *Times* newspaper; it makes no extravagant demands as a creed ; its whole value and significance lie in its appropriation by act and practice.   It is not likely to be very popular with either the philosophers or religionists of to-day.

On the 21st of March, Lord Collingwood writes to Lady Collingwood, off Cadiz, as follows :—

" I have at present no prospect of sending a letter, but I begin this because I love to write to you; and I know that were it only to tell you I am well, it would be gladly received. If some of those French who are flying about do not come hither soon, I shall get horribly tired of sauntering here, with the thousand causes of care and anxiety in other quarters. I have many in search of their squadrons, and shall ever hope—for could we but once meet them again, I doubt not that we should make as complete a business as the last was. At least, you may depend upon it, your husband will leave nothing in his power undone to make you a countess : not that I am ambitious of rank, but I am to be thought a leader in my country's glory, and to con-

tribute to its security in peace. I wish some parts of
Hethpoole could be selected for plantations of larch, oak,
and beech, where the ground could be best spared.
Even the sides of a bleak hill would grow larch and fir.
You will say that I have now mounted my hobby; but
I consider it as enriching and fertilising that which
would otherwise be barren. It is drawing soil from the
very air. I cannot, at this distance, advise you on the
education of our darlings, except that it should not stop
for a moment. They are just at that period of their
lives when knowledge should be acquired; and great
regard should be had to the selection of the books which
they read, not throwing away their precious time on
novels and nonsense, most of which might be more fitly
used in singeing a capon for table, than in preparing a
young lady for the world. How glad I should be just
now to have half-an-hour's conversation with you on
these important subjects! I have, indeed, a great deal
to say to you. Here are several officers with me very
much in distress that they cannot get home; but what
can I do? The Admiralty will not say a word to me
about the prizes, the promotion of officers, or any subject.
I never did, nor ever will I do anything but what I
think conducive to the public good. I am not ambitious
of power or wealth more than I have, nor have I con-
nexions of any kind to sway me from the strict line of
my duty to the country. I have neither sons nor cousins
to promote by any of those tricks which I have ever
held in contempt; so that when I err it will be from
my head, and not my heart. It is not everybody that
is so indulgent as you are in their judgment of my poor
head, but there is no one by whose judgment I can be
so much flattered. I have not heard from Lloyd's

Coffee-house about the seamen: all that happened in October seems to be an old story, and I must get something ready for a summer's rejoicing—something airy."

In a letter addressed to Lady Collingwood, shortly after the above was written, Lord Collingwood gives a very sad account of the death of a young officer. He says:—

"I have written to Lloyd's about Mr. Chalmers' family. He left a mother and several sisters, whose chief dependence was on what this worthy man and valuable officer saved for them from his pay. He stood close to me when he received his death. A great shot almost divided his body: he laid his head upon my shoulder, and told me he was slain. I supported him till two men carried him off. He could say nothing to me, but to bless me; but as they carried him down, he wished he could but live to read the account of the action in a newspaper. He lay in the cockpit, among the wounded, until the *Santa Anna* struck; and, joining in the cheer which they gave her, expired with it on his lips."

Thus one more true heart amongst the unnumbered ones that ceased to beat for the welfare of their country and their race on this stern occasion was for ever stilled, unconquered and unconquerable in the destruction of its mortal part, witnessing that the old heroic spirit still survived, and making death itself immortal.

On the 5th of April we find Lord Collingwood.

giving directions to Lady Collingwood on the education of their children during their journey to London.
He says, "I wish that in these journeys the education
of our children may not stop; but that, even on the
road, they may study the geography of that part of
England through which they travel, and keep a
regular journal, not of what they eat and drink, but
of the nature of the country, its appearance, its
produce, and some gay description of the manners of
the inhabitants." He particularly charges them to
visit the tomb of Nelson on their arrival in town, and
requests they may be shown everything of interest in
the great city.

One cannot help being struck with the different
notion of education for his daughters held by Collingwood from what is usual and general now in his class
of society. If his views were not quite exceptional,
how different must the aspect of society have been
in his day! No slang, no tinsel manners, no arrogance, no vapid accomplishments at the expense of
a solid education; everything calm, dignified, and
sound in basis. The young gentlewoman of his time
may have possessed less varied information and fewer
useless accomplishments than the young lady of to-
day, but she must have had more intelligence, a better
knowledge of the womanly function, and been infinitely more useful at the head of a household. In
some respects, indeed, circumstances are vastly

altered. It would be regarded as an amusing piece of extravagance if a young English lady of the present day were asked to keep an account of her experiences during a journey from Edinburgh to London; to note down the aspect and products of the country, together with something of the character and manners of the people of the districts passed through, seeing that her knowledge of the former would be limited to a glimpse here and there out of the window of a railway carriage going at a flying speed, and that of the latter to the officials of the railway stations at which the train might happen to stop. Not that such a journey need be altogether barren, though I imagine to most young people of the present time their experiences of travel would be limited to the contents of a newspaper, a magazine, or the pages of the last new novel; but how different, at the best, from the same journey undertaken at the beginning of the century! It is true that we do not consider how much we have lost by such a change of circumstances. Travelling in England, in any intelligent sense of the term, may be said to be practically destroyed. An Englishman, as a rule, knows nothing really of his country now, excepting at certain points and places. Of its roads, its quiet villages, its smaller towns, its most characteristic nooks, and the quaint traits of character which are always developed in secluded localities, he is, on the

whole, quite ignorant. Undoubtedly such experiences
are a very great loss, and no doubt many of the
superficialities of modern society are fostered and
encouraged, if not actually caused, by the indifference
with which people learn to regard everything excepting the immediate object they have in view. The
varied circumstances, the features of the country, the
aspects of the towns and villages on the road, the
distinctive marks of character to be observed in the
different persons and classes continually met with,
both on the journey and at the inns where stoppage
was necessary, would in former times, in travelling
the length of England, have furnished a most interesting piece of study, and been a most valuable
adjunct to education. Human nature cannot be
studied now as it was formerly studied. Not only is
a Shakespeare, but even a Fielding, a Smollet, or a
Hogarth, utterly impossible now. All this has been
fully recognised and commented upon in some
quarters with considerable bitterness. But in spite
of sentimental regrets, sensible and judicious people
will turn their eyes to the compensations. If one
page in the history of society is closed, another is
open. The field of study—study of the most interesting sort—has been widely extended. Convenience,
decency, and comfort must count for much. Our age
is superficial, ugly, and sadly wanting in simplicity,
thoroughness, and probity; but it is not without

promise, and society may hereafter learn those more important lessons which it thinks proper to regard with the most culpable indifference now.

A very marked instance of the difference between the impetuosity of Nelson and the more deliberative and conciliatory character of Collingwood is afforded in a correspondence which took place on the right of taking water and stores into the British ships on the coast of Portugal, which was in treaty with England during the war, and had maintained a strict neutrality. Shortly before the battle of Trafalgar, Lord Nelson wrote a letter to Lord Strangford, the British representative at Lisbon, to complain of the treatment of the English ships at Lagos. It appears that the French consul stationed at that port had stretched his prerogative to the extent of inducing the Portuguese to limit the English ships in the supply of water and provisions, and went so far as to cause the Portuguese sentry to threaten to fire upon the English if they presumed to take more than the prescribed quantity. It will be interesting to place two of these letters side by side, as illustrative of the diversity of character and policy of these fine-spirited men. Nelson writes from the *Victory*, under date October 3rd, 1805. After describing the situation of affairs with some degree of repetition, he says,

" Now, what I demand is, that our officers and men, whilst in the neutral port, shall be under the protection of the neutral flag, and not be permitted to be insulted by the interference, either secret or open, of our enemies; and that every ship which goes into Lagos, or other ports, shall have such refreshments as are reasonable. . . . I shall send a ship or ships to take in water at Lagos. They shall wash, or let it run overboard, if they please; and I rely that the Portuguese Government will direct that our enemies shall not insult our people, much less dictate to the Portuguese Governor for his treatment of us. However degraded the Portuguese may allow themselves to become, it is hardly fair that they should expect us to be insulted by our enemies on their neutral ground: for if, by words or any other mode of warfare, they do permit it, I shall certainly retaliate."

Here we have all the fire and energy of Nelson's character, the impetuous desire to rush at once into action. Lord Collingwood's letter to Lord Robert Fitzgerald on the same subject is couched in more temperate language. Whilst he fully recognises the unwarrantable nature of the conduct of the Portuguese, he, at the same time, considers the difficulty of their position, and strives rather to avert a quarrel than to enter into one. His letter is as follows:—

" I have received the honour of your lordship's letter of the 17th, enclosing a note which had been written to you by the Portuguese Government, than which nothing can surprise me more. It is a complaint made where they confess that no offence has been given.

"I have long been fully sensible of the jealousy
entertained by the French of our ships being supplied
with refreshments from Portugal; and anxiously
desirous that nation between which and Great Britain
so long and so faithful a friendship has subsisted,
should not be subjected on that account to disagreeable
discussions with our enemy, I have forborne to send
ships to their ports. Those that have been at Lagos of
late were merely there by chance, for the purpose of
refreshing their crews. It is reported to me that they
have been supplied; but not in that free and liberal
manner to which, by treaty, the subjects of His Majesty
have a right, and which is due to the friendship and
affection which have been so long established between
the two countries. Instead of the free use of the
market, where they might furnish themselves with
fruits and fresh provisions, they have been limited to a
portion insufficient for half the crew; and even the
number of casks of water which they were to have
has been determined.

"If by the other means of being supplied to which the
minister of Portugal alludes, is meant that of taking
such supply by night, I did give strict orders that no
such illicit correspondence should be held. What is
due to neutrality we have a right to receive in the face
of day. If Portugal be unhappily in such a situation
that she must veil her friendship, and look sternly on
those whom she was wont to welcome with open arms,
her misfortune is to be deplored; but I never will allow
the dignity of the British flag to be questioned by the
ships engaging in an intercourse which will not bear to
be looked upon by the whole world. That our thus
declining supplies because the mode of furnishing them

was considered as derogatory to the dignity of the British name, should be considered as an infringement of the most strict neutrality, is what I do not comprehend; and I should suspect that there must have been some misapprehension by the officer at Lagos, and that he has stated his own mistaken ideas instead of the fact.

"The same motive, of not giving to our enemies any cause of complaint against those whom I have considered our friends, determined me not to avail myself of the right of sending squadrons into their ports, nor was ever such a measure in my contemplation."

It will thus be seen that Collingwood was just as determined not to compromise the honour of the English navy as Nelson had been, and whilst exerting the most reasonable forbearance towards the Portuguese until they should be able to act independently, he, at the same time, would consent to nothing underhand or surreptitious in his dealings with them. I find the following upon the same subject amongst his unpublished despatches :—

"The proposal of Mr. d'Arango I conceive to be in every point of view inadmissible. In the first place, no collection of cattle or refreshment could be made so secretly as to escape the vigilance of the Spaniard and his emissaries; but if they could, it would completely compromise the dignity of the British flag to have our ships lie off this port like smugglers, to receive by stealth in the night supplies which by treaty they are entitled to purchase in common with other neutral powers. I do not mean cargoes for a fleet at sea, but the refreshments and water for the ships which go there: nor is it necessary that this secret mode of supply should be resorted to while Barbary affords better cattle at perhaps a lower price, until Portugal can ·assert her right to sell her commodities to whom she will."

How distinctly illustrative of the best English feeling is this fine perception of an open behaviour: the hatred of anything like concealment or disguise: the frankness which courted the day and feared no disclosures, because it had no unworthy secrets! One of the most prominent traits in Collingwood's character was its entire freedom from anything like duplicity. He had no need to hide himself behind false or specious appearances, because he had nothing of which to be ashamed. His whole nature sought the light. His creed did not belie his practice. The serpents, hypocrisy and insincerity, never found a dwelling within his breast. How eminent such a position! What a strong citadel does he inhabit who dwells within the entrenchments of candour and sincerity,—

> " Whose armour is his honest thought,
> And simple truth his utmost skill!"

He needs no factitious supports to maintain his reputation, for it stands secure on immovable foundations; he is saved all the paltry disguises and miserable expedients of concealed motives and a deceptive behaviour. With him there is no twilight region between right and wrong; there is nothing dubious, hazy, or wavering in their limitations, or mistakable in their proportions. The haggling compromises of a mercenary casuistry have no meaning for him—they are a dead letter; their fatal and illusive spells have no power to paralyze his moral sense and blunt the edges of pure living; he breaks their insidious meshes as a lion would burst the toils of a spider; he does not count the shades or weigh the relative value of evil thoughts or evil actions; he aims deeper: he gets rid of them all; he banishes the whole untoward brood. To admit the measuring and appraising of sins and wrongs would be to make a compromise with them, to recognize their implied right to be there, as it were, in some form or other; but with the confident transparency of an assured Christian valour, with the heroism of one who really loves and lives in what is good and right, with the fine instinct of a soul devoted to the service of truth, duty, and God, he banishes all, all; and lifting his brow to the sun, meets the gaze of the angels without a blush.

In the April of 1806, Lord Collingwood removed his flag from the *Queen*, which he had occupied six months, to the *Ocean*, one of the finest ships of the line. His private affairs, relating to the property which

had been left to him by his relative, pressingly
demanded his attention. In fact, there was every
personal reason why he should wish to return home;
but he disregarded them all. On his removal to his
new ship, he writes to Lady Collingwood :—

"My sister wrote to me on the necessity of my going
home to direct my private concerns in the North ; but
they seem so insignificant to the duty I have to do here,
that I cannot even think of them. I have not heard
enough about them to be able to give any direction on
the subject, but I daresay my brother will take care that
everything proper is done . . . I hope you told my
darling how delighted I was with her French letter :
she must converse when she has an opportunity, and
remember not to admire anything French but the
language. I wish I could collect something in the fleet
to amuse you, but we are all very grave. The only
subject that gives a gleam of cheerfulness is the hope
that the fleet in Cadiz may venture out again; they
will soon be strong enough. I have only been ten days
in port since I left England. It would weary anything.
Would that we had peace, that I might laugh again,
and see you all merry around me."

Another letter, showing his generous consideration
and large-minded conscientiousness of principle, was
addressed to Mr. Blackett, on the 1st of May, from
which the following is an extract :—

"I am much obliged to you for the information you
give me about Chirton, and I wish that the very letter
of the will of my deceased friend should be observed.

Whatever establishments may be found there for the comfort of the poor, or the education and improvement of their children, I would have continued and increased. I want to make no great accession of wealth from it, nor will I have anybody put to the smallest inconvenience for me. I shall never live there; nor were it as many thousands as it is hundreds, would I quit my present situation to regulate it. I hope the butler and servants are provided for. Smith, the man I have now, is a gentleman in manners and education; and he will, I daresay, see me out as my own servant."

Such words as these reconcile one to humanity, and give fresh confidence in the human heart. They fill one with gladness to think that pure, elevated, and disinterested principle may still find a home amongst men—has not quite fled from the face of the earth for ever. Such sentiments are sent like spiritual sunshine from heaven, that we may not be altogether chilled and frozen in the world's cold ways, nor be changed to marble by its hard maxims and cruel practice. How true is the Christianity which they express! How do they breathe the tone and spirit of the Christian gentleman! Lord Collingwood was not one who could spend one day in religious observances and grind the faces of the poor to the dust the next. He was not one of the noisy and talkative class of philanthropists who do everything for their fellow-creatures but help them. He was not one of those who preach the vanity of riches, and love and treasure them as the dear life. He could afford to lose money or do without it, but having it, he could not afford to lose the opportunity of beneficence. The truth is, that although the sweetest and most innocent pleasures of life were denied to himself—the common blessings of home and domestic enjoyment—he loved to see every one in comfort about him, and to distribute happiness and contentment wherever he was able to do so.

A further instance of his generosity is given in a letter addressed to Mr. Blackett on the 7th of November :—

" We are going on here in our usual way, watching an enemy who, I begin to suspect, has no intention of coming out, and I am almost worn down with impatience and the constant being at sea. I have devoted myself faithfully to my country's service ; but it cannot last much longer, for I grow weak and feeble, and shall soon only be fit to be nursed and live in quiet retirement; for having been so long out of the world, I believe I shall be found totally unfit to live in it. But I do not care ; I trust my dear Sarah and my daughters will be kind to me, and I shall look no farther for comfort. I have for some time past desired to send a gift to the charitable institutions at Newcastle in token of my respect for my countrymen ; but a letter from my bankers, informing me that the stream was dry, prevented my doing it before ; but now I transmit 100*l.*, of which I wish to subscribe 20*l.* for the monument of my worthy master, Mr. Moises, and to present the remaining 80*l.* to the Fever and Lying in Hospitals, Dispensary, and Infirmary."

In the same spirit he says, on another occasion,

"I am very much obliged to you for the trouble you have been so good as to take about Chirton and the colliery. I have but little information on the subject, and am so far removed that I cannot give particular directions; but, as a general principle, I wish, that in the changes which the working this colliery may make, as few of the people who are established in the houses belonging to me, and of respectable character, should be removed as possible. Let them have the offer of such public-houses as are, or may be vacant; but I do not think it would be common justice to turn out those already established: nor would I consent to it for any increase of rent, however great."

It is very sad to think that whilst half the world was being gladdened by the voices of spring and the fresh green of the new year, and the flowers were springing in the Morpeth garden, and the oaks beginning to swell at the bud, only no renovating influences should have found their way into the narrow ship's cabin where the duty-devoted admiral worked his weary life away. His home waited for him, his wife and daughters waited for him, his oaks and old Scott awaited him, his private affairs required his presence; he was growing old in the yoke: why could he not go where there was every personal inducement to attract him? His country

never valued his services as they ought to be
valued. He would receive no kind of repayment
adequate to his toil and self-denial. Would others,
under the same circumstances, do what he was
doing? All these considerations surrounded him and
were set quietly aside, they never influenced his
conduct for a moment. He knew that the first
object of life ought not to be personal happiness,
and that it never could rightfully become so in the
present condition of the world: that, in fact, it must
lie a great way from selfish happiness. He knew that
as long as a great proportion of mankind was occupied
in creating mischief and disorder, there could be
little rest for the good man; and that he must
labour, and sacrifice, and die at his post, if needful, and
look for no reward, no recompense, but that which
his work carried with it and in it. He must be content to maintain the grand old laws, and be crushed
under them if necessary; but never abandon them.
He must take his stand on the strong foundations,
and let everything go by him rather than relinquish
them. He must, if need be, lash himself to the
mast, and, like the undaunted Vasco da Gama, in
the epic, confront the tumult with an unshrinking
resolution and defy the spirit of the storm.

On the 2nd of May he writes to Mrs. Moutray as
follows:

" If I write you but a little letter, receive it kindly,

for my days and nights are too short to get through my business. I work like a Turk, till I am stupefied with the mixture and variety of things which pass through my brain. You have heard, I daresay, that my kinsman at Chirton is dead, and has left me that estate. If I were at home I should make it three thousand a year. But when shall I go home? Never.

"At present the rentals are twelve or fourteen hundred pounds. The coals are its chief value, and they cannot be worked till I return; but I shall not go back the sooner for that. I am living here but miserably, with every kind of inconvenience, and give up every thought of personal comfort while I can serve."

What a splendid sermon is contained in these words! Most persons "serve" in order to enjoy personal comfort some time or another, or for some ulterior purpose or object—for wealth, honour, popularity: but for service' sake, for the sake of doing their duty alone, how many serve? How many are there who hold service to be its own reward, and look to no other? How many are there who "give up every thought of personal comfort while they can serve?" Lord Collingwood did not ask whether his services were appreciated or not. This never weighed so much as a straw in governing his motives or conduct, either in relaxing his perseverance or strengthening his energies for the work he had taken in hand, which he felt to be necessary for the well-being of his country, and humanity at large. He did not say, I give up every thought of personal comfort that I may be applauded. He did not give up personal comfort that he might be great or honoured. He had had salutary experience, both actual and by observation, of the rate at which true patriotism, self-immolation, and conscientious rectitude were valued by his country. He did not give up every personal comfort that his name might go the round of the newspapers and furnish a topic for the gossip of the clubs. Reputation—the bubble reputation—much greater reputation—might have been had at an infinitely less cost. It might have been had with the ease of taking his place in the legislature of his country, by uttering a few cheap phrases in the popular vein—talking about great deeds instead of doing them. But not for any of these did he give up the comfort of his days and nights: it was to "serve." No basker in the sunshine of opinion, no truckler to the breath of a gossamer praise: no; but though his country might overlook his services, though his fellow-men might disregard them, though the very heavens clouded over him, blotting out the sun and peace from his life; yet he could raise his face to the realms above the cloud and above the thunder, and say, I serve. Whilst others talk, whilst others lie, cheat, steal, and call themselves honest men, I serve. Am I sick, not in body alone, but in mind also, of the worst sort of sickness, the sickness of the heart, the sickness that comes of hope deferred; am I weary; is my soul ready to faint beneath the burden? Do the pleasant ways of life lie in the far distance—in a region which I shall never reach? Do the days bring me toil and the nights no rest? What matter! I can serve. Here is my anchor and my stay, the bread of my soul and the sustenance of my spirit, the rainbow of my life, the star of my path, the substance of my hope and the sum of my desire. Everything else is as nothing whilst I can serve.

"Did they think," says Collingwood to Admiral Grindall, in allusion to a report that he was about to retire, "that one day's good service is enough for my share, or that having a comfortable home, I should think it enough to take care of myself? If they did, they are strangers to me. While we are at war and I am able to serve, I shall not flinch."

As the *Ocean* lay off the Straits of Gibraltar, Lord Collingwood was applied to by the King of Naples for assistance in the protection of Sicily. This was granted, with the following sound recommendations:

" The population must be animated to its defence, not merely by the example of the British troops, but by the nobility and gentry engaging in the service of their sovereign, and bearing the fatigues of war in common with the people, to whom an interest should be given in the preservation of the state, by ameliorating their condition by every possible means. Self-interest is a powerful stimulus, which pervades all human nature.

Make those by whom the work must be performed at last, and who alone can give security and permanence to what is done, more happy: give them a more perfect security for their property than they can hope for by any change, and their hearts will engage in the service, and Sicily be secure against the efforts of the enemy."

This excellent advice was based upon the political axiom that no nation can become great which depends upon the arms or assistance of others for its elevation or support. What is true of the individual is true of the state also. Stability and power can only be had by the exertion of individual and independent energy. They can never be conferred by external agencies. In this respect the race is certainly to the swift and the battle to the strong. A people enslaved to passion, to indolence, and to indifference can never form a great state or commonwealth. No natural advantages, no sustenance of foreign powers can bestow strength and tension upon its nerves or infuse spirit into its movements. The people whose souls are free can have no conqueror. For a moment they may wear the fetters, but it is only to shake them off; for a time liberty may veil her head from them, but it is only that she may emerge the brighter for the obscuration. It is not stone walls which can make the prison, nor iron bars the cage of an enfranchised spirit whose natural home is in the realms of freedom, who is faithful to the sacred brotherhood of temperance, honesty, and truth.

At the end of May Lord Collingwood complains that his body grows weak and his limbs lady-like. He also begs Lady Collingwood not to talk about the wound in his leg, lest people might think he is vapouring about it. A letter which he wrote to Lady Collingwood in the middle of June is interesting as further illustrative of his principles and sentiments. He says,

"'This day, my love, is the anniversary of our marriage, and I wish you many happy returns of it. If ever we have peace, I hope to spend my latter days amid my family, which is the only sort of happiness I can enjoy. After this life of labour, to retire to peace and quietness is all I look for in the world. Should we decide to change the place of our dwelling, our route would, of course, be to the southward of Morpeth : but then I should be for ever regretting those beautiful views which are nowhere to be exceeded : and even the rattling of that old waggon that used to pass our door at six o'clock in a winter's morning had its charms. The fact is, whenever I think how I am to be happy again, my thoughts carry me back to Morpeth, where, out of the fuss and parade of the world, surrounded by those I loved most dearly and who loved me, I enjoyed as much happiness as my nature is capable of. Many things that I see in the world give me a distaste to the finery of it. The great knaves are not like those poor unfortunates, who, driven, perhaps, to distress from

accidents which they could not prevent, or, at least, not
educated in principles of honour and honesty, are
hanged for some little thievery; while a knave of
education and high breeding, who brandishes his
honour in the eyes of the world, would rob a state to
its ruin. For the first, I feel pity and compassion; for
the latter, abhorrence and contempt: they are the
tenfold vicious. Have you read—but what I am more
interested about, is your sister with you, and is she
well and happy? Tell her—God bless her!—I wish I
were with you, that we might have a good laugh.
God bless me! I have scarcely laughed these three
years. I am here with a very reduced force, having
been obliged to make detachments to all quarters. This
leaves me very weak, while the Spaniards and French
within are daily gaining strength. They have patched
and pieced until they have now a very considerable
fleet; whether they will venture out I do not know: if
they come, I have no doubt we shall do an excellent
deed, and then I will bring them to England myself.

How do the dear girls go on? I would have them
taught geometry, which is of all sciences in the world
the most entertaining: it expands the mind more to
the knowledge of all things in nature, and better
teaches to distinguish between truths and such things
as have the appearance of being truths, yet are not,
than any other. Their education and the proper
cultivation of the sense which God has given them are
the objects on which my happiness most depends.
To inspire them with the love of everything that is
honourable and virtuous, though in rags, and with
contempt for vanity in embroidery, is the way to make
them the darlings of my heart. They should not only

read, but it requires a careful selection of books; nor
should they ever have access to two at the same time;
but when a subject is begun, it should be finished
before anything else is undertaken. How would it
enlarge their minds if they could acquire a sufficient
knowledge of mathematics and astronomy to give them
an idea of the beauty and wonders of the creation. I
am persuaded that the generality of people, and particularly fine ladies, only adore God because they are
told it is proper and the fashion to go to church; but I
would have my girls gain such knowledge of the works
of the creation, that they may have a fixed idea of
the nature of that Being who could be the author of
such a world. Whenever they have that, nothing on
this side the moon will give them much uneasiness of
mind. I do not mean that they should be stoics, or
want the common feelings for the sufferings that flesh
is heir to; but they would then have a source of
consolation for the worst that could happen."

With such sentiments of wisdom and thoughtfulness did this good man keep his heart alive, and
strive to instil into others the large principles by
which he was himself governed. In half sportive
fashion he writes to Mrs. Moutray a little afterwards:—

" I do indeed rejoice with you, and most heartily congratulate you on the marriage of your daughter, which
I hope will add so abundantly to your happiness as to
leave you nothing in this world to ask for. I have
heard all that could be said on the subject of peace, but
have never for a moment changed my opinion of the
subject. While Buonaparte lives, or until France meets

with some great reverse of fortune, we shall never have peace. I have ordered my girls to be put upon the war-establishment for their lives, and to be taught to darn their own stockings, so that at all events they may not be tattered; for there is no knowing what the prosecution of the war for half a century may bring us to. And yet I am convinced that there is less danger in it than in the insidious peace which he would make. Whatever happens, I think it can make no change to me. I must have food, and I am sure I have nothing else that can be called a comfort.

"You, my dear madam, can easily believe that all those additions to my honours and fortunes (and I would not be thought ungrateful for them), have added nothing to my happiness; in some instances they have interfered with it. My habits were formed before; and when at home I was as contented with my lot in the world as any creature could be. Whatever turns me from the course in which I have found my pleasures will be irksome to me. Pray may a peer plant cabbages; or would digging a few potatoes soil my dignity? In truth, it should not, more than running down a poor hare, or shooting an unfortunate partridge in the midst of his brothers and sisters. My wife is, I hope, enjoying herself at Newcastle; and she ought, poor thing, to have something to make her amends for the loss of her husband."

The long blockade duty upon which Collingwood was now occupied, which was looked upon as insignificant by outsiders, taxed his powers to the utmost; for he had not only the dissatisfaction of personal inaction united with all the responsibilities of an unceasing watchfulness, but he had a ship's crew to maintain in good order and spirits, with all the dangers incident to a stagnation of occupation when disaffection was a prevalent source of disorder in the fleet. He says to Mr. Blackett, in a letter dated off Cadiz, December 9th, 1806 :—

"I have little to tell you from here; the enemy's squadron are quite ready for sea, but in the upper part of the harbour, out of the way of storms; while we contrive to watch them, that they may not go out without an encounter. A battle is really nothing to the fatigue and anxiety of such a life as we lead. It is now nearly thirteen months since I let go an anchor, and for what I see it may be as much longer. They are increasing their navy daily, while ours is wearing out."

Indeed, the duties which make the least noise in the world are often the most arduous, perhaps almost always so. True heroism does not necessarily lie in remarkable deeds, and is certainly not limited to them. It is not confined to, perhaps, in its highest phase, is hardly represented by, the storming of forts, the facing of cannon mouths, the flashing of swords, and the rattling of rifles; it is not only found amidst carnage and bloodshed, rolled in smoke and swathed in slaughter; for these may be faced and fought through by sheer animal force and ¦circumstantial excitement; but it lies rather in supporting manfully the long weary march, in watching through the spirit-chilling picket, in the round of eventless and monotonous duty. In its noblest phase it is decorated with no medals, bears no insignia, has no titles, is frequently not known or recognised beyond itself. To do great deeds with a world looking on, ready to applaud and incite, many have found not difficult; but to meet the great struggle of duty against self-interest and inclination, without hope or desire for recognition or reward; to stand erect and firm when there are none to look on with words of praise or honour, or even in the face of indifference or ridicule, as sometimes happens; to maintain an unflinching rule, an undeviating and independent course of action, may well challenge the best spirit of the bravest man, and lay upon courage itself the weight of an inexpressible sadness.

Whilst Sir Sidney Smith kept the French in check on the coast of Calabria, the Spaniards were, as Collingwood states, endeavouring to fit out another fleet at Cadiz. Nevertheless, Lord Howick, as a measure of security, thought it expedient to send Collingwood to the former, Sir John Duckworth being left to occupy the latter station. It was to his great regret that at this time Lord Howick, with whom Collingwood's relationship had been highly satisfactory, was displaced at the Admiralty. Intelligence and punctuality in the direction of the naval

affairs of the kingdom had been so deplorably deficient, that the loss of any one possessing these qualities
was the more seriously felt. For whatever great
deeds distinguished our navy during these stirring
times, they were certainly not due to the government,
at home, but were rather accomplished in spite of it.
If England had had no better and more disinterested
men at sea to look to in her critical emergencies than
those who, for the most part, composed her direction
at home, she must have sunk beneath the waves of
oblivion, and never again have risen above them.

Lord Collingwood was always thinking of somebody or something else beside himself. His thoughtfulness even extended to posterity. Dreamless of
the uses which would be made of steam and iron, he
was, as has been already said, particularly anxious
for the growth of oak timber. He writes to Mr.
Blackett at this period :—

" The scarcity of timber for our ships is daily increasing, and I am afraid my oaks will not be of sufficient
growth for the supply of this war. I have written a
letter to old Scott to inquire about my trees and
garden."

What a delightful incident is this! In his oaks
he does not forget the friendly hands in whose care
they were left. He does not send a message, for
that would not be equal to the importance of the
occasion. He writes a letter, which old Scott will

read for himself. If all Collingwood's communications had received the attention which, no doubt, this letter received, how much would his labours have been lightened? I should like to have peeped over the old man's shoulder as he read it, and to have seen the smile which came over his face. How his eager fingers would tremble as he opened it! He would never touch it without first wiping the mould from his hands; but in spite of that, it would get very brown before he ceased to carry it in his pocket. I should not wonder if the corners and foldings became worn through with repeated opening and reading before he was warned to wrap it up in paper and deposit it in the most sacred place in the house; but not until he had learnt every word of it by heart, although he would, of course, always pretend to have forgotten it, in order that he might have the pleasure of producing it before his cronies on Sunday afternoons, as they discussed the news of the war, and settled all the affairs of it to their own perfect satisfaction.

Lord Collingwood had a very faithful friend and adherent on ship-board, whom he often mentions. It was his dog, Bounce, already introduced to the reader, who seems to have taken wonderfully to seamen's ways, and to have shared his master's vicissitudes in a most sympathetic manner; although, it must be confessed, he never loved the sound of warfare. When Collingwood was elevated to the peerage, Bounce did not forget himself, or the occasion. "I am out of all patience," says Collingwood, "with Bounce. The consequential airs he gives himself are insufferable. He considers it beneath his dignity to play with commoners' dogs. This, I think, is carrying the insolence of rank to the extreme; but he is a dog that does it." Bounce had his function, too, and fulfilled it quite as well as, indeed, better, than many of higher pretension. Collingwood, speaking of the inefficiencies of a young midshipman, says, "He is of no more use here, as an officer, than Bounce is, and not near so entertaining." Indeed, Bounce, it would appear, was no unintelligent companion, for, if he did not say much, he could listen attentively. "I shall miss Admiral Grindall very much," said Bounce's master, in one of his letters, "for he has been a companion for my evenings; and when he is gone I shall only have Bounce to talk to." After a time, Bounce began to feel the confinement of ship-board and want of exercise almost as much as his master; but, unlike his master, he became rather spoilt by it. He required, and obtained, little indulgences to keep him in heart and spirits. He ceased to gambol, subdued by the cares of service, so that he had to be coaxed and petted, and even with these, was often mopish, sad, and melancholy, grew fretful and dainty,

M

and did not sleep well of nights; so his master set a
song to music, and sang him to sleep. "Tell the
children," he says, in one of his letters, " that Bounce
is very well, and very fat, yet he seems not to be
content, and sighs so piteously these long evenings,
that I am obliged to sing him to sleep, and have sent
them the song :—

> " Sigh no more, Bouncey, sigh no more,
>   Dogs were deceivers never ;
> Though ne'er you put your foot on shore,
>   True to your master ever.

> " Then sigh not so, but let us go,
>   Where dinner's daily ready,
> Converting all the sounds of woe
>   To heigh, phiddy-diddy."

Poor Bounce ! He became old in the service. He
was to have had his portrait taken, but, somehow or
other, this did not happen : so that his lineaments
will be lost to posterity. He died at his post; not
on the couch of ease, not in his master's cabin, where,
doubtless, he would have had every attention ; but
on a stormy night in the boisterous ocean. He had
been taught to run on the main chains, and one dark
night, thus exercising himself, fell into the sea and
was drowned. Every one who has loved a dumb
animal, which has returned his affection, will understand what sort of a loss this was to Collingwood in
his situation at that time. We hear little about it

directly, but its painful nature is reflected in a letter
to him from his cousin, Mrs. Hughes, who writes, in
December, 1809 :

"What shall I say about Bounce? I am really more
sorry than I ought to be for an animal. I always heard
of Bounce when any one came from you; and all had
some little story to tell about him. I do indeed lament
with you over him."

The poor animal appears to have lost his life only
a short while before the death of his master.

The policy of the French had been all along to
maintain as full and efficient a fleet as possible, and
always to remain in port under the protection of the
batteries; thus compelling the English to a continual
watchfulness, and to wear out their ships at sea in
the most wearying and dispiriting inaction. By this
means the enemy had hoped, as has been already
stated, to exhaust the energies of the English, and
then to enter upon their own course of action. In the
meantime, the Napoleonic dynasty pushed itself, by
force of arms, in all directions. Every kingdom in
Europe, except England, stood in fear of the power of
the Corsican, or was already subjugated by his yoke.
The philosophic sagacity of Collingwood foretold
what then lay closely veiled in the bosom of the
future, and of which there were no visible indications, that as his rule was " repugnant to the interests
and welfare of the people," so whenever the tide of

his greatness should be at the full, "his ebb would be more rapid than his rise," and adds, "I cannot help thinking that epoch is not distant." There were, however, few signs of it at that time. Almost all Europe was in a tumult. The King and Queen of Prussia, driven from the throne, had been reduced to the necessity of seeking shelter at the shop of a tradesman. Collingwood's observations on this circumstance are so apposite, that they deserve to be quoted. He says :—

"The poor King and Queen of Prussia in an apothecary's shop! How reduced! And unable to get their breakfast until the bed is made! What a fall for greatness. This, however, is but the humiliation of the body, subject to chances and changes as a condition of its being; 'subject to the skyey influences that do it hourly afflict.' But, if his mind be still upon his throne, he may, even in an apothecary's shop, devise the means of rescuing his distressed country from its present thraldom. Gustavus Vasa planned the emancipation of his country among the iron-mines of Dalecarlia. Charles XII. did not feel himself less the monarch when a stone kitchen was his palace, and cooks and grooms of his council. If the king possesses mind and talents, and by justice, and a strict regard to their happiness, has gained the affections of the people, his case is not hopeless."

In the midst of the harassing duties which pressed him on every side, it is refreshing to find him writing this delightful letter to Mrs. Moutray. It will not be necessary for me to point out the charm and elegance of its style, and the purity and elevation of sentiment which make it a model of this species of composition. It was begun on the 17th of February, 1807, whilst he was still off the coast of Spain, not long before he left for the East.

"I received last month your letter of September, for our post is neither very regular nor speedy. Your description of your habitation delighted me. It is the sort of scene in which I should like to pass the few days I have yet to see; where, retired from the bustle and vanities of the world, I might, in a small circle of amiable and sensible friends, give loose to affections that mark the fair side of human nature, and descend the hill of life with composure and comfort. I wish your neighbourhood were as agreeable to you as your home; but the world was not made for us alone. Nature delights in variety, and there is as much in the manners, the pursuits, and the pleasures of men and women, as in any other of her works. You have seen as much of that variety as most people, and know the wisdom of conforming to the manners and adopting the habits of those among whom our lot places us. What is new, in time grows supportable, and in another short time pleasurable; and I should not wonder if you were soon to get a little pad of a horse yourself, and examine more nearly into the delights of the chase which makes your neighbours who engage in it so very joyous. For myself—what can I tell you of myself, but that I am well in health, and my mind miserably harassed? Month after month I am upon the full stretch. No-

thing has gone wrong with me; but the anxiety and
dread lest anything should happen, in despite of my
cares, keep me for ever serious, for ever bent.   I do not
know the day that I have smiled, and see no prospect
of this war ending; then, indeed, I could be merry.   I
suppose, if ever I come on shore, I must live at Chirton.
It is only half in the country, and my house at Morpeth
and the country about were so much to my taste, that I
shall leave them with regret.   Chirton has many con-
veniences that I had not, but I had enough to be very
comfortable and very happy.   It is fifteen months since
I was last in port.   I shall not be fit for anything after
this."

"*March* 17.—I had written the above letter some time
before your last kind one came to me: kind as it was
it made me very sorrowful; it had so much the tone
of taking leave that my spirits sank while I read it.   My
spirits are not gay and cheerful, as they once were.
Wherever you go you will have my prayers that every
happiness and comfort may be yours, and that you may
live to see your daughter as happy as the world's best
gifts can make her.   They are to be found at home or
nowhere.   For my own part, I can say that I have
never been perfectly happy since I left planting my
cabbages and excellent potatoes, and then, I think, I
was as near it as any human creature had a right to
expect.   As to the bit of wood, I wish I could send
you one of the beams of the *Prince of Asturias* to cut
up into tea-chests; and if I get hold of the Cadiz
gentlemen, I certainly will remember your commission.
I left the *Royal Sovereign* before the smoke was out of
her, and since that they have cut away all the old
timber, that seems so valuable to you, my dear friend,

and made chips for the bakers of it. But why would
you store your memory with an event that must cause
more of pain than pleasure; it is a story grown faint in
the recollection of most people. Admiral Grindall told
me he arrived at Portsmouth the anniversary of that
day, and it was no more remembered than the battle of
La Hogue. Fame's trumpet makes a great noise, but
the notes do not dwell long on the ear. As to my
picture, my face is not fit for it; for care sits heavy on
my brow, and time has furrowed my cheek. Picture
me in your mind; it is there I wish to be drawn, such
as I am, and preserved, rather than in gilded frames in
a back parlour. Tell your dear Kate and Mr. De Lacy
that I wish them every happiness, and that when I
hear they are enjoying it, I shall rejoice. I hope you
will excuse these crosses, but I thought it were pity to
send two letters together. If they are difficult to read,
remember it is a world we must bear crosses in; and I
hope these will be the extreme of yours."

Amidst much political bungling, in which Collingwood's judgment was ignored, his knowledge
disregarded, and his perplexities increased by uncertain and conflicting orders, an expedition was
despatched to the Dardanelles, which joined the
Russian fleet there in order to compel Turkey to
adhere to the terms of the triple alliance into which
she had entered with Russia and England against the
French power, which she had infringed by her
vacillating conduct. Constantinople and the Dardanelles were blockaded under difficult and dangerous

circumstances, when a little careful diplomacy would
have secured the object in view, Turkey having all
along displayed a friendly disposition towards England,
with whom she was willing to treat, although more
shyly disposed towards Russia. These things weighed
heavily on the mind of the admiral. Writing to Mr.
Blackett, on the 14th of June, 1807, he says :—

"Our miscarriages at Constantinople and misfortunes
at Alexandria have worn me to a thread. I am so-so in
health—not ill. My labour is unceasing and my vexations many; but I cannot help them. My eyes are
weak, my body swollen, and my legs shrunk to tapers;
but they serve my turn, for I have not much walking."

In a letter to Lady Collingwood, after describing
in a graphic manner an Oriental dinner to which he
had been invited in company with the Capitan
Pacha and the Pacha of the Dardanelles, he writes
as follows :—

"How glad I should be, could I receive a letter from
you, to hear how all my friends are! for I think the
more distant they are the more dear they become to me.
We never estimate the true value of anything until we
feel the want of it, and I am sure I have had time
enough to estimate the value of my friends. The more
I see of the world, the less I like it. You may depend
on it that old Scott is a much happier man than if he
had been born a statesman, and has done more good in
his day than most of them. Robes and furred gowns
veil passions, vanities, and sordid interest that Scott
never knew."

Although Collingwood was placed amidst so much that was uncongenial to him, and although in his letters to his most intimate friends he did not refrain from telling his troubles and annoyances, it must not be supposed that he indulged in a sour or gloomy disposition, or that he habitually wore a long face or bore a heavy heart under his burdensome duties. This was far from being the case. Lord Collingwood's temperament, like that of most thoughtful and reflective natures, was reserved and retiring. His real character and disposition were unknown to all who had not a more or less intimate acquaintanceship with him. His moods were not gloomy, but the reverse. He loved to lighten his toil with pleasant jests and cheerful sallies. He often indulged in a pun. A certain gravity of manner gave zest to his jokes, which are described by more than one person as having been pointed and effective. A few of these have been preserved. The first gunpowder which was given to the Spaniards at the commencement of their revolution having been fired away in honour of one of their saints, when they applied for more, Collingwood told them he should give them no more, unless they promised to reserve it for sinners and not for saints. Once, when he saw preparations being made for illuminating the town of Cadiz for the celebration of some dubious advantage gained in a petty skirmish with the French, he said, "I thought their victory was a somewhat doubtful and dark affair, but now, I suppose, they are going to throw some light upon it." These and other pleasantries which are related of him, though not remarkable in themselves, are evidences of the geniality and cheerfulness of his character. The extracts from his correspondence here given, as having a more special bearing on his personal character, are only a small part of what he wrote, and are frequently separated by long intervals; so that the mention of his trials and difficulties must not be taken as implying anything like a persistent dwelling upon them. Nothing was further from Collingwood's nature and character than a tone of habitual complaint. He neither indulged in it himself nor encouraged it in others. The reader will have observed in all the extracts given in this volume the entire absence of anything like stricture or animadversion upon those persons or bodies of persons under whom it was his duty to act, just as there was never the least unwillingness or hesitation in carrying out whatever orders were given, although, as he says, he did not refrain from stating his opinion upon them when they were unnecessary or injudicious. It must be noted also that, with trifling exception, it is only his later correspondence, and that which was written during the most depressed portion of his life, which has been preserved. Of his youthful gaiety, cheerfulness, and elasticity, there is no record beyond the fact of their having existed. But this, perhaps, we can best spare, as the genuine and fundamental soundness of his character could not be attested so efficiently by any evidence derived from his early life as by that of a later period, when years of experience and painful trial had assayed the serviceable temper of his principles and proved the inviolable persistency of their nature.

On the 26th of December, 1807, he writes to his children as follows:—

"My dearest children :—A few days ago I received your joint letter, and it gave me much pleasure to hear that you were well, and I hope improving in your education. It is exactly at your age that much pains should be taken ; for whatever knowledge you acquire now will last you all your lives. The impression which is made on young minds is so strong that it never wears out ; whereas everybody knows how difficult it is to make an old snuff-taking lady comprehend anything beyond Pam or Spadille. Such persons hang very heavy on society ; but you, my darlings, I hope will qualify yourselves to adorn it, to be respected for your good sense and admired for your gentle manners. Remember that gentle manners are the first grace which a lady can possess. Whether she differ in her opinion from others or be of the same sentiment, her expressions should be equally mild. A positive contradiction is vulgar and ill-bred ; but I shall never suspect you of being uncivil to any person. I received Mrs. Moss's letter, and am much obliged to her for it. She takes a lively interest that you should be wise and good. Do

not let her be disappointed. For me, my girls, my
happiness depends upon it; for should I return to
England and find you less amiable than my mind
pictures you, or than I have reason to expect, my heart
would sink with sorrow. Your application must be to
useful knowledge. Sarah, I hope, applies to geometry,
and Mary makes good progress in arithmetic. Independently of their use in every situation in life, they are
sciences so curious in their nature, and so many things
that cannot be comprehended without them are made
easy, that were it only to gratify a curiosity which all
women have, and to be let into secrets that cannot be
learned without that knowledge, it would be a sufficient
inducement to acquire them. Then do, my sweet girls,
study to be wise.

" I am now at sea, looking for some Frenchmen whom
I have heard of; but I was lately at Syracuse, in Sicily.
It was once a place of great note, where all the magnifi-
cence and arts known in the world flourished: but it
was governed by tyrants, and a city which was twenty-
two miles in circumference is now inconsiderable. Its
inhabitants have great natural civility; I never was
treated with so much in my life. The nobility, who
live far from the court, are not contaminated by its
vices: they are more truly polite, with less ostentation
and show. On my arrival there the nobility and senate
waited on me in my ship. Another day came all the
military: the next the vicar-general, for the bishop was
absent, and all the clergy. I had a levee of thirty
priests—all fat, portly-looking gentlemen. In short,
nothing was wanting to show their great respect and
regard for the English. The nobles gave me and the
officers of the fleet a ball and supper, the most elegant

thing I ever saw, and the best conducted. The ladies were as attentive to us as their lords, and there were two or three little Marquisinas who were most delightful creatures. I have heard men talk of the *dieux de la danse*, but no goddesses ever moved with the grace that distinguished the sisters of the Baron Bono.—God bless you! my dear girls."

To Lady Collingwood he writes in an elevated strain, which bears the true patriotic ring : for we know that its grand words were no mere boast, no empty vapouring, but the language of settled and earnest purpose, supported by the devotion of every energy and confirmed by every act of his life. He says :—

" I am just now cruising with my fleet off Maritimo, and intend continuing here until I get information to lead me to the French, which I expect very soon, and then hope that God will bless me. Our country requires that great exertions should be made to maintain its independence and its glory. You know, when I am earnest on any subject, how truly I devote myself to it ; and the first object of my life, and what my heart is most bent on (I hope you will excuse me), is the glory of my country. To stand a barrier between the ambition of France and the independence of England is the first wish of my life ; and in my death, I would rather that my body, if it were possible, should be added to the rampart, than trailed in useless pomp through an idle throng."

Collingwood's whole efforts were now given to

meet with the French fleet, which had left Toulon, and was in the Mediterranean. But this was very difficult. All communication with the Continent was stopped. The French took care to spread false reports of their movements wherever any little information might have been gleaned. Collingwood sailed from port to port only to learn that the enemy had already left. Upon the sea there was no possibility of getting information. Trade had totally ceased: the seas were a waste as far as commerce was concerned. Not a single ship was to be seen; only the English line and its frigates despatched hither and thither in search of the enemy or intelligence of their movements. Whilst Collingwood was watching Sicily, which he believed to have been the real object of the French cruise, the French made their way by the coast of Africa and returned to Toulon in safety. This was a severe blow to the indefatigable English admiral. His utmost efforts had been repaid by disappointment. He knew that success was the only criterion of popular judgment, and whilst every effort was baffled, felt himself powerless to do more. Once he was only a single day's sail from the fleet without knowing it. This preyed upon his mind deeply; for he felt he had missed a chance which might have resulted in an important, perhaps decisive, engagement. Added to this, the defections of officers and want of right management in the ships were a source of constant trouble and anxiety. The navy became to a great extent the pension of incompetency and the instrument of office. Collingwood wrote to the Earl of Mulgrave, at that time at the head of the Admiralty, saying that it was certain he could not know many of those who were appointed to command at the importunity of friends, as some of them had to be dismissed. Great difficulty was found in manning the fleet. Inefficient landsmen were sent, totally unfit for the sailor's duties. Lord Collingwood had suggested that young boys of from fourteen to sixteen years of age should be trained and sent out, as they soon became efficient sailors, but the government at home was slow to take up the suggestion, even when it had been found to answer. By such unworthy and miserable mismanagement Collingwood was impeded in his movements, harassed in his direction of the fleet, and every obstacle thrown in the way of an easy and orderly government.

He thus describes the position of affairs at this time to the Earl of Northesk. His letter is dated, off Toulon, May 18, 1808:

"We have dissensions and bickerings in Parliament at a time when all the wisdom and energy should be employed in counteracting and diverting this silent torrent that overwhelms states, as if they had no firmer foundation than a haycock, and sweeps them away to

be no more heard of.   The consequence is, that ministers are so taken up by repelling attacks in Parliament,
that it is impossible they can have time for repelling
the attacks of the enemy ; so that those measures which
ought to be kept most secret are left to the conduct of
inferiors in office, and the first you hear of them is in a
newspaper.   Now, if the agents of Buonaparte were in
those offices, they could not manage his interest better.
Does not all the world know that one man can keep a
secret better than two.   I do assure your lordship that
those contentions and my own ill-luck in not having
fallen in with the Frenchmen are sometimes like to
break my heart: it is the consciousness that I have
left nothing undone which was in my power that
supports me, and the hope that I still entertain, that
all will yet be well.   I was at Syracuse when I heard
they were come into the Mediterranean, and sailed the
morning following, the 23rd February, to assemble the
fleet off Maritimo.   The first I heard of them was that
they had passed Pantellaria on the 15th, and that
account was but vague : from every quarter a different
statement came.   I have been pursuing them from
point to point ever since, often in doubt whether I
was going right or wrong.   The French are all now in
Toulon, the Spaniards starving at Minorca.   Sicily or
Turkey is their object, and whenever they move,
I hope for ample satisfaction for my disappointment.
They already outnumber us at all points, and so much
depends on our meeting soon, that I am impatient.
The affairs of Spain are curious ; that dynasty is done,
or I am mistaken.   A Frenchman will be on the throne
of Spain within these six months ; probably Murat,
the prince of something, who married Buonaparte's

sister! I am weary of recounting the wickedness of that—I feel compunction in calling him man.

"And so God bless you, my dear lord."

When Napoleon had emptied Spain of the best men in it, by draughting them off upon foreign service; after exhausting the armaments of the Spaniards and draining their arsenals, seizing their king and placing his brother Joseph on the throne, the whole nation rose in arms, and at once allied themselves with England to get rid of the intruders. Collingwood entered into treaties with them, gaining their confidence by plain-dealing and uprightness of conduct in every transaction, so that he was afterwards consulted upon all important occasions; very much facilitating the subsequent operations of Wellesley in the Peninsula, when the war became a military rather than a naval one. The Spaniards received from England money, arms, ammunition, and whatever was required to get rid of their oppressors and to restore their country to freedom and independence.

Under the weight of so many cares and such ceaseless labours, altogether too much for one person to bear, Lord Collingwood's constitution began to give way. After enduring almost to the limits of endurance, he made application to be released from service on the 2nd of August, 1808, to which the Earl of Mulgrave made the following reply:

N

" I read with great uneasiness and regret the concluding part of your letter, in which you express some doubt of the continuance of your health to the end of the war, and I earnestly hope that the service of the country will not suffer the serious inconvenience of your finding it necessary to suspend the exertion of your zeal and talents. It is a justice to you and to the country to tell you candidly, that I know not how I should be able to supply all that would be lost to the service of the country, and to the general interests of Europe, by your absence from the Mediterranean. I trust you will not find the necessity, and without it, the whole tenour of your conduct is a security that you will not feel the inclination, to quit your command while the interests of your country can be so essentially promoted by your continuing to hold it."

This, however, flattering as it might be, brought no additional strength to meet his difficulties. Vital power was flowing from him, sensibly oozing away. Once more he wrote to the Admiralty, formally desiring to be released from service until his health should be re-established ; saying that he did so with reluctance, but hoping they would be satisfied that his application proceeded from the same sense of public duty which made him formerly desire to serve. At the same time, August 26th, 1808, he wrote to the Earl of Mulgrave as follows :—

" As my strength and health are very much impaired, and as I attribute it in some measure to the long time I have been at sea, and to the anxiety of mind which I continually feel for the service, I have very reluctantly written to the Admiralty to pray that their lordships will be pleased to relieve me. But sentiments of public duty demanded this from me, and at every period of my life the public service has been paramount to all personal considerations. When I am recalled, it would be a great satisfaction to me if your lordship would promote one or two of my lieutenants. They are respectable officers, and will be creditable and useful to the service. Your lordship knows how little opportunity I have had of serving them; most of them have been with me near three years, and the only one whom I have advanced, Captain Clavell, was made on the death of Captain Secombe."

To this letter he received a reply of fair words which sealed his fate. It was dated from the Admiralty, September 25th, 1808, as follows:—

"I have received with great regret your private letter of the 26th of August, explaining to me the grounds on which your public letter, requesting to be relieved, had been written. I lament to learn that your health and strength have been impaired from the long and uninterrupted exertions by which you have so ably conducted the delicate, difficult, and important duties of your command. Upon a former intimation of the injury which your health had received, I took the liberty of pressing strongly upon your lordship's consideration the importance which I attach to your continuance in a situation in which, through a variety of great and complicated objects, of difficult and delicate arrangements of political as well as of professional considerations, your lordship had in no instance failed to adopt the most judicious and best-concerted measures. Impressed as I was and am with the difficulty of supplying your place, I cannot forbear (which I hope you will excuse) suspending the recal which you have required, till I shall hear again from you, whether, under the diminished difficulties of your command, you are still of opinion that a longer continuance at sea would be injurious to your health, which I should feel it a public as well as a personal duty to consult. Should such be your determination, I am not without hopes that the service may yet derive material advantage from the exercise of your lordship's talents, without any impediment to the restoration of your health, if the eventual proposal which I am about to submit to your lordship should be consistent with your arrangements, and receive your assent. I have it in contemplation to relieve the officers commanding the several ports, who have been more than three years on that duty, and in making my arrangements, I should consider it as highly advantageous to the service if your lordship would take the direction at Plymouth, which is, in a great degree, the centre and spring of the most active points of naval operations. I shall await your lordship's answer, in the hope that I may have the advantages of your able assistance in one or other of the two commands—at Plymouth, if the Mediterranean should no longer be consistent with the material consideration of your health.

" Upon receiving the names of the lieutenants whom your lordship is desirous of promoting, I shall pay attention to your wishes in that respect."

At last, it would seem, his country had begun

dimly to perceive his value, and, as the result of it determined to work him to death. For the beast of burden, overtaxed and overwrought, there is rest, the earned repose; but for him there was none. One would have thought that from a man of Collingwood's character, who had given so many instances of his bravery and indefatigable devotion, the first word or breath of a desire for recall on the ominous score of health would have been listened to as significant; one would have thought that a common knowledge of the inefficiency of overwrought powers would have demanded consideration, if it had been only on the narrow principle of mere economy of service; but all such considerations were disregarded. What did it matter as long as the lovers of office could maintain a situation of popularity at his expense? They did not feel his sufferings. They were not racked by his overstrained nerves, or depressed by his debilitated system. As long as the back which carried the burden was not broken, what to them was the toil which bore its wearisome weight day by day uncomplainingly? Then they sought to silence him with paltry bribes. The generosity which had prompted him to ask the merited promotion of worthy officers, and never ceased to ask it, was at last listened to. The simplest act of justice, in which Collingwood had no personal interest whatever, was granted as a favour; and another sop was added, which, however honourable in itself, could be of little value to the worn-out admiral as long as he was confined to the narrow limits of a ship's cabin, shut out from everything which could make life pleasant or agreeable : he was made Major-General of Marines, in the place of Lord Gardner, who had died.

The very candour and unexaggerated terms in which his reply to the above letter is conveyed should at once have excited the gravest suspicion of his ability to continue his duties. It is as follows:—

" I have received the honour of your lordship's letter of the 6th of September, and it has afforded me the highest gratification to find that the conduct I have observed in the several occurrences that have presented themselves to my attention has met your lordship's approbation.

"I can always assure your lordship of my zeal and diligence in my duty, and of the exercise of my best judgment in the service of my king and country. I never have had, I hope I never shall have, a desire to shrink from it, while I have health and ability to perform it : but my life has been a long one, and an anxious one to a mind which never engages in anything with indifference. I have not any particular illness ; but am become exceedingly weak and languid, and often find myself too much disordered to exert myself as I wish to do, and as my situation requires. It was this consideration that induced me to make the request to the Board of Admiralty, which I have done since in writing to your lordship—and now that I have explained my motive and reasons, I have only to add, that my best service is due to my country as long as I live, and I leave all else to your lordship's consideration and convenience."

Of course, all this was of no avail. No doubt the circumstances of Collingwood's condition were dismissed with the occasion. Once more he sat down to his desk, once more he devoted his jaded powers to the cares of office. The aching head and weakened hand were disregarded ; new energies were summoned, and obeyed the call, but every one of them was a draft drawn on the nearly exhausted resources of life ; the herald and harbinger of death. His next letter to the Earl of Mulgrave, so pathetic in its manly resignation, says more than a thousand complaints. It is dated from the *Ocean*, at Malta, January 10th, 1809 :—

"In the last month I received the honour of your lordship's letter of the 25th September. Nothing could be more gratifying to me than such a testimony of your lordship's approbation of the measures which I have taken to promote the public welfare on the several occasions which have come within my cognizance. My long continuance at sea has made me very feeble ; and the fear of my unfitness, which I know people are often the last to discover in themselves, induced me to make the application. My situation requires the most vigorous mind, which is seldom possessed at the same time with great debility of body. Since my letter of the 30th October to your lordship on this subject, the

vexations which I have had on account of the affairs
in Catalonia, and the violent stormy weather, which has
done much injury to some of the ships, particularly to
the *Ocean*, have increased my infirmity : but on this
subject I have nothing to add to what was said in that
letter. I have no object in the world that I put in compe-
tition with my public duty ; and so long as your lordship thinks it proper to continue me in this command,
my utmost efforts shall be made to strengthen the impression which you now have ; but I still hope, that whenever it may be done with convenience, your lordship will
bear in mind my request.   On the subject of Plymouth,
I have only to say, that wherever I can best render my
service, I shall be at your lordship's command. I would
not have requested to be called from hence on any
account but that which I have stated; and when my
health is restored, I shall be perfectly at your lordship's
disposal ; but with the little I ever had to do with ports,
I should enter on that field with great diffidence."

Before this, he had written to Lord Radstock :
"My weak eyes and feeble limbs want rest; my
anxious breast has not known an hour's composure
for many months."

Upon Lord Collingwood, as upon every thoughtful
and unselfish mind, the burden of the world and its
wrongs sat heavily. Too nearly interested in all that
went on around him, the miserable shifts, chicanery
and untrustworthiness which he constantly witnessed,
filled his soul with indignation and disgust.   So much
did he feel this, that sometimes he could have been

content quietly to leave a world so full of confusion, of wrongs which he could not redress, of abuses which he could not remedy; in which the lines of right and wrong, to him so distinctive and clear, were so inextricably entangled and obscured as to make the very time itself appear to be hopelessly and irretrievably out of joint. In a mood inspired by such circumstances, he writes to Lord Radstock on the affairs of Spain: "These subjects, and my cares for · them, are wearing me to death; but much that I see in the world reconciles me to its approach whenever it shall please God. If men were honest and just, all difficulties would be overcome; but of those very people who are conducting the defence of their country, one scarcely knows whom to trust."

On the 17th of June, 1809, we find Collingwood writing a tender letter to his wife, off Toulon, from which the following is an extract:—

"I am writing you a letter, my love, because there is nothing I so much delight in as a little communication with her on whom my heart for ever dwells. How this letter is to go to you, I know not. I never hear from your world, and cannot tell whether anything from ours ever reaches you; but I take the chance of sending you my blessing. I am pretty well in health, but have fatigue enough: nothing that is pleasureable ever happens to me. I have been lamenting our ill-luck in not meeting the French ships the only time, perhaps, that they will show themselves out of port for the summer; but

it was not to be avoided; they never come out but with
the good assurance of being safe. Now that the French
fleet is destroyed at Rochefort, they may surely select
some officer to relieve me, for I am sadly worn. Tough
as I have been, I cannot last much longer. I have seen
all the ships and men out-two or three times. Bounce
and I seem to be the only personages who stand our
ground."

Perhaps there is nothing that shows more clearly
the true temper and genuine quality of Collingwood's
nature than the inability of bodily depression, weariness, and disappointment to poison or sour it. It is the
privilege of only the noblest natures to undergo the
resignment of their dearest hopes, desires, and feelings and to be improved by it. Gold is refined, not
consumed, by fire, and of such a temper was the
nature of this good man. His deprivations and adver-
sities were never visited on others. He had learnt
sympathy by the necessity for the exercise of self-
denial, and was never made hard or callous by it.
He had conned life's lessons well, and had taken their
moral to heart. He could not be comfortable himself
unless every one else was so by whom he was surrounded, and if others were happy, it alleviated his
own pain. At the time of his application to be
allowed to retire, he writes to Lady Collingwood: " I
am not ill, but weak and nervous, and shall think
seriously of going home, for the service I am on
requires more strength of body and mind than I

have left in my old age; and in future I shall think only of my comforts, and how best I can make everybody about me comfortable and happy." With the same exemplary consideration he says of his servant, Smith: "I hope Smith will stay with me when I go on shore, for he is quiet and well educated, and suits me very well. I have not had occasion to find fault with him these four years; indeed, never." Surely it is a fact of great significance that he had had a servant with whom he had never found fault during so long a period. However dutiful and attentive the man may have been, how many are there who, being placed under the trying circumstances of Lord Collingwood's later life, would have forborne fault-finding; who would not have imagined something wrong in the best service? Nothing is more conspicuous, indeed, in the character of Collingwood than its absolute justice. He would go out of his way unlimitedly, and spare no expense or trouble to remedy an injustice, either private or public. A mild and temperate behaviour opened the way for the exercise of this fine quality. Passion had no mastery in him, but was the bondslave of reason and judgment. "Justice is always in danger," he said, "when temperance is wanting." It is very noticeable, also, that as he grew older, his mind expanded in the elevations of a large philosophy, reminding one of the mental experiences and conclusions of the wisest men, as Aristotle, Epictetus, and Marcus Antoninus. He had learnt to appraise personal energy at its right value, and to understand its just limitations, so that intention and purpose were not weakened by frustration, nor expectation disappointed by failure. "The power that God has given me," he says to Lord Radstock, "I exercise to the utmost: for that I am accountable—beyond that I am not." When, in writing to Mrs. Moutray, he characterises it as a proof of wisdom, "that you are well and happy, enjoying the good that is in your power, and not lamenting the absence of that over which you have no control," he gives utterance to the best part of philosophy, measured by the highest standards of reason and a wise judgment. He had also learnt, to quote his own expression, the use and value of "the patient courage which waits for the opportunity it cannot create."

On the 8th of November, 1808, he writes to Lady Collingwood, off Toulon, as follows:—

"You cannot conceive how I am worried by the French; their fleet is lying in the port here, with all the appearance of sailing in a few hours; and God knows whether they will sail at all; for I get no intelligence of them. Their frigates have been out in a gale of wind, were chased by some of our ships, and got in again. We have had most frightful gales, which have injured some of my ships very much; but now that the Alps have got a good coat of snow on them, I

hope we shall have more moderate weather. I have a
double sort of game to play here, watching the French
with one eye, while with the other I am directing the
assistance to be given to the Spaniards. The French
have a considerable force at Barcelona and Figueras, by
which they keep the avenues open for Buonaparte to
send his army whenever he is ready. The Spaniards
have much to do, more than the people in England are
aware of. I have, however, from the beginning given
the ministers a true view of the state of affairs in Spain.
It is a great satisfaction to me to find that everything
I have done has been approved by Government; and the
letters I receive from the Secretary of State always com-
municate to me His Majesty's entire approbation. I
have heard from the Governor of Cadiz and others, that
some of my papers, addressed to the Junta of Seville, on
the conduct which the Spaniards ought to pursue on
certain occasions, have been very much commended.
Perhaps you may think I am grown very conceited in
my old age, and fancy myself a mighty politician; but
indeed it is not so. However lofty a tone the subject
may require and my language assume, I assure you it
is in great humility of heart that I utter it, and often
in fear and trembling, lest I should exceed my bounds.
This must always be the case with one who, like me,
has been occupied in studies so remote from such
business. I do everything for myself, and never distract my mind with other people's opinions. To the
credit of any good which happens I may lay claim, and
I will never shift upon another the discredit when the
result is bad. And now, my dear wife, I think of you
as being where alone true comfort can be found, enjoying in your own warm house a happiness which, in the

great world, is not known. Heaven bless you; may
your joys be many and your cares few. My heart often
yearns for home; but when that blessed day will come
in which I shall see it, God knows. I am afraid it is
not so near as I expected. I told you that I had
written to the Admiralty, that my health was not good,
and requested their lordships would be pleased to relieve
me. This was not a feigned case. It is true I had not
a fever or a dyspepsy. Do you know what a dyspepsy
is? I'll tell you. It is the disease of officers who have
grown tired, and then they get invalided for dyspepsy.
I had not this complaint, but my mind was worn by continual fatigue. I felt a consciousness that my faculties
were weakened by application, and saw no prospect of
respite; and that the public service might not suffer
from my holding a station and performing its duties
feebly, I applied for leave to return to you, to be
cherished and restored. What their answer will be, I
do not know yet; but I had before mentioned my
declining health to Lord Mulgrave, and he tells me in
reply, that he hopes I will stay, for he knows not how
to supply my place. The impression which his letter
made upon me was one of grief and sorrow: first, that
with such a list as we have, there should be thought
to be any difficulty in finding a successor of superior
ability to me; and next, that there should be any
obstacle in the way of the only comfort and happiness
that I have to look forward to in this world. The
variety of subjects, all of great importance, with
which I am engaged, would puzzle a longer head than
mine. The conduct of the fleet alone would be easy,
but the political correspondence which I have to carry
on with the Spaniards, the Turks, the Albanians, the

Egyptians, and all the states of Barbary, gives me such constant occupation, that I really often feel my spirits quite exhausted, and, of course, my health is much impaired: but if I must go on, I will do the best I can. The French have a force here quite equal to us; and a winter's cruize, which is only to be succeeded by a summer one, is not very delightful, for we have dreadful weather; and in my heart I long for that respite which my home would give me, and that comfort of which I have had so little experience.

I hope your father and sister are well, and far happier than I am; but tell them that, happy or miserable, I shall ever love them. ——, who was making a fortune, has behaved so ill that he is to be tried by a court-martial; but there are some people who cannot bear to be lifted out of the mud; it is their native element, and they are nowhere so well as in it."

A noticeable expression in this letter is worth dwelling on for a few moments, as indicating a very distinctive part of the character of Lord Collingwood. He says, "I do everything for myself, and never distract myself with other people's opinions." Collingwood was characterised, in common with all great-minded persons, with the most firm decision of character. He deliberated carefully, weighing every contingency which his sagacity and forethought presented to him, and never overlooked anything of importance which it was possible for him to foresee. When he sent Sir John Duckworth to the Dardanelles, the directions he gave were

written with the utmost care. After reading his
orders, the admiral returned to the cabin, and asked
what he must do in case of certain occurrences.
" Read your orders," said Collingwood, " and if you
do not understand them, come to me and I will
explain them." The orders were re-read. Everything had been anticipated, and the admiral retired
perfectly satisfied. His was no " appended mind,"
that worked on the will of another. He stood upon
his personality, and looked for no support stronger
than his own resolution. His decisions were not
influenced from without; they were always self-
generated and reached by thoughtful processes. He
did not await events, and allow them to guide him ;
but determined his course of action and forestalled
the occasion. He did not postpone his conclusions,
but thought out everything to a definite issue, so as
to require no after consideration, unless under a
change of ruling circumstances. His resolutions
formed, they were as good as accomplished: he
dispensed with self-questionings, and never flinched a
hair's breadth from carrying them out. He did not
talk about his plans, nor delight in their discussion,
well knowing that many words have the tendency
to take the pith out of purpose and make execution
linger. Another noticeable quality in his decisions
was that they were never tinged with the least
personal feeling ; there was no smack or savour of

individual interest to be traced in them; self was ignored and forgotten; whatever other benefit they might design or include, his own was never consulted from first to last in any of them.

It is not easy to appraise this sort of resolution at its full worth. It is so rare, that diamonds are more common. The possessor of it—the master of himself and ruler of his own life—has a treasure indeed. Nations may become bankrupt of their forces, but he shall retain his; dynasties may fall, but he shall stand; the seasons may go over him, carrying all their vicissitudes with them, but the white blossoms of an auspicious spring shall fill the garden of his soul, nor shall their fruit be promised in vain. You must be either hammer or anvil, says the German sage. You must either steer or be steered. You must either have a purpose of your own, or be the sport of circumstances, a feather in the wind, the tool and instrument of others. How few are they who seize the materials of life, and, by a bold and vigorous effort, mould them to their will! Yet unless we do this, we lose the highest privilege of humanity, we utterly relinquish our title to the heroic or the divine. If you wish to claim your birthright, you must start with this principle: I will do something, I will be something, and nothing shall hinder me from accomplishing that which I have determined. To an energetic will, everything is flexible; its power is

o

not defined or prescribed; adamant becomes plastic
in the hands of an invincible resolution.   To abandon
the helm of determination, to drift on to the shoals of
indifferentism, to let the fitful wind of opinion rule the
courses of irresolution,—what greater misfortune can
befal a human soul?   Better fight against the rocks
and perish on them than that; better buffet the
waves till they overwhelm us than that; better breast
the storm till the hand grows numb and the brain
palsied, than let strength of decision ooze away in
languid inaction, and firm resolve perish shamefully
at the foot of baulked and ineffectual desire.

Perhaps the following letter and its advice,
addressed to his daughter by Lord Collingwood, from
Malta, on the 5th of February, 1809, may be considered old-fashioned and obsolete by the most
advanced young ladies of the present day; but it is
to be hoped that there are those still amongst us to
whom it will appeal with all the force it had upon
the day when it was written.   For, indeed, the constitution of true breeding is always the same, modes
and fashions do not alter it; it is elementary in its
nature and unchangeable in its essence; it is without the conventions of time and place; it is fixed
and permanent; it is like the beauty of a Greek
statue—beautiful through every age, and unaffected
by whatever circumstances it may be surrounded.
What an intimate and exact knowledge of the most

refined properties of gentleness, courtesy, and the high behaviour which distinguishes and dignifies human nature at its best do these lines discover! For my part, I cannot but coincide with every word of them. Such characters as they seek to model may be counted old-fashioned by the disciples of convention, change, and externals, but it is pleasant and refreshing to meet them, and when one does so, one heartily wishes the world contained more of them. We do not remark the want of modern accomplishments in such as these; nay, I am not quite sure but that we congratulate ourselves on their absence. The letter is as follows:—

"I received your letter, my dearest child, and it made me very happy to find that you and dear Mary were well, and taking pains with your education. The greatest pleasure I have amidst my toils and troubles is in the expectation which I entertain of finding you improved in knowledge, and that the understanding which it has pleased God to give you both has been cultivated with care and assiduity. Your future happiness and respectability in the world depend on the diligence with which you apply to the attainment of knowledge at this period of your life, and I hope that no negligence of your own will be a bar to your progress. When I write to you, my beloved child, so interested am I that you should be amiable, and worthy of the friendship and esteem of good and wise people, that I cannot forbear to second and enforce the instruction which you receive, by admonition of my own, pointing out to you the great advantages that will result from a temperate conduct and sweetness of manner to all people, on all occasions. It does not follow that you are to coincide and agree in opinion with every ill-judging person; but after showing them your reason for dissenting from their opinion, your argument and opposition to it should not be tinctured by anything offensive. Never forget for one moment that you are a gentlewoman; and all your words and all your actions should mark you gentle. I never knew your mother—your dear, your good mother—say a harsh or a hasty thing to any person in my life. Endeavour to imitate her. I am quick and hasty in my temper; my sensibility is touched sometimes with a trifle, and my expression of it sudden as gunpowder: but, my darling, it is a misfortune which, not having been sufficiently restrained in my youth, has caused me much pain. It has, indeed, given me more trouble to subdue this natural impetuosity than anything I ever undertook. I believe that you are both mild; but if ever you feel in your little breasts that you inherit a particle of your father's infirmity, restrain it, and quit the subject that has caused it until your serenity be recovered. So much for mind and manners; next for accomplishments. No sportsman ever hits a partridge without aiming at it; and skill is acquired by repeated attempts. It is the same thing in every art: unless you aim at perfection, you will never attain it; but frequent attempts will make it easy. Never, therefore, do anything with indifference. Whether it be to mend a rent in your garment, or finish the most delicate piece of art, endeavour to do it as perfectly as possible. When you write a letter, give it your greatest care, that it may be as perfect in all its parts as you can make it. Let the subject be sense, expressed in the most plain, intelligible, and elegant manner that you are capable of. If in a familar epistle you should be playful and jocular, guard carefully that your wit be not sharp, so as to give pain to any person; and before you write a sentence, examine it, even the words of which it is composed, that there be nothing vulgar or inelegant in them. Remember, my dear, that your letter is the picture of your brains; and those whose brains are a compound of folly, nonsense, and impertinence, are to blame to exhibit them to the contempt of the world, or the pity of their friends. To write a letter with negligence, without proper stops, with crooked lines and great flourishing dashes, is inelegant; it argues either great ignorance of what is proper, or great indifference towards the person to whom it is addressed, and is consequently disrespectful. It makes no amends to add an apology for having scrawled a sheet of paper, of bad pens, for you should mend them, or for want of time, for nothing is more important to you, or to which your time can more properly be devoted. I think I can know the character of a lady pretty nearly by her hand-writing. The dashers are all impudent, however they may conceal it from themselves or others; and the scribblers flatter themselves with the vain hope, that, as their letter cannot be read, it may be mistaken for sense. I am very anxious to come to England, for I have lately been unwell. The greatest happiness which I expect there, is to find that my dear girls have been assiduous in their learning.

"May God Almighty bless you, my beloved little Sarah, and sweet Mary too."

How tender and impressive are these warm phrases! How naturally they seem to burst from a heart charged with every dear remembrance, with every fond parental wish! There is something almost pathetic in the writer's remarks on his own character and disposition. He felt the burden of mortality weigh heavily upon him; but it was not made the subject of demonstrative exercitations. His faults were kept for correction, not for discourse and expatiation. He schooled himself; for his own mastership failing, to what mortal should he go for a master? He knew it was of no use—indeed, might be harmful—to talk of his faults. The only available thing was to amend them; to fight them and conquer them on the sole battle-field upon which they could be effectually met, that of the heart which had given them birth.

Another noticeable part of this letter is the recommendation to do everything in the best manner possible, however trifling the thing may be in itself. It is noticeable, because it was in a great measure owing to this property of conscientious thoroughness in all he did that Lord Collingwood rose to the elevation of character and rank as a commander which he attained. He had learned the art of doing everything well; for he knew it was the passport to success. He knew that it is by a successive series of touches, each insignificant in itself, that perfection is reached; that the noblest building rises through imperceptible gradations, and that every worthy work of art is the sum of infinitesimal elaborations. And, indeed, what is habit, but an accumulation of the most minute acts, thoughts, and purposes, each one of itself quite inconspicuous and apparently unimportant? Yet we know that the sum of the habits thus formed constitutes character, and character is the measure of the man. The mode in which these trivial circumstances have been seized and dealt with implies and includes the whole difference between a base man and a hero. It is a thought perhaps too little dwelt upon, that we are every single moment of our lives occupied either in raising ourselves, in elevating the soul into the large, clear regions of intellectual freedom and absolute law, or in lowering our nature, in depreciating every lofty standard, in forging the fetters which will eventually bind us hand and foot, in clipping the wings of the spirit, and abridging its divine soarings to the narrow compass of a restricted and constrained mortality, and in shutting out the heavenly vision by the cares and wants of the body with a thousand distractions. It is for this reason that every great and rightly ambitious soul is anxious to set the seal and impress of a lofty purpose upon everything that it does, knowing that as is the material of the contexture, so will be the piece that is woven. A trivial thing becomes great when done thoroughly and from a high point of view, whilst to absolute thoroughness of doing and living there is no measure wide enough to assign the grand proportions.

On the 15th of June, 1809, Lord Collingwood writes to Mrs. Moutray, from the *Ville de Paris*, off Toulon, as follows:—

"I wish most sincerely you had been surprised by seeing my flag scudding into Spithead, but I now begin to think you never will. When I applied to go home, it was really not from a pining for the enjoyment of my own domestic comfort, though I believe no creature ever possessed more ; but from a consciousness that I was not equal to contend with the vexations, and conduct the multiplicity of complex and for ever varying affairs that present themselves to my direction. I have laboured incessantly, and with all the industry I am capable of; but I feel, I am sensible that I am not able to get over it as I used to be, and am always in arrears. You know, my dear madam, how much pleasure I ever have in complying with your requests: you are too good and too wise to make any that do not include the public benefit as well as the gratification of a friend. Lieutenant Bourne is the very officer who ought to be in a frigate, and I consider it as a piece of good fortune that he has been pointed out to me. He is appointed to the *Spartan*, commanded by Captain Brenton, one of the best frigates and best officers in the station, and, as good luck would have it, employed on a most active service. You make me smile, my dear friend, by your observation on the great assailants of friendship, but I hope they are not founded on an accurate knowledge of the world. You have been living a recluse life in that archdeaconry, and reading queer books of odd people. Do you think people's minds change with their condition, and that what appeared fair and good when my eyes were clear and penetrating, should be less so in my idea, because their sense is now dim and weak? In truth, my head aches just as it used to do, my limbs are far more feeble, and the sweet sleep that old Scott the gardener enjoys, when he has not a fit of rheumatism, seldom comes to my lot; my best consolation is, that the kindness of those I esteem and regard will never be impaired. I know little of the politics of the times, and they tell me there is a comfort even in this. I have heard, however, what has made my heart ache; but I mind my fleet. I did once wish to have my daughters succeed me in my title, but the more I have thought of it, the less important it appears. I would ennoble their minds by a virtuous education, which is much more important, but my long absence from England is a misfortune to them."

Lord Collingwood's ship, the *Ocean,* having suffered severely from the gales of the preceding winter, he shifted his flag, for the last time, to the *Ville de Paris,* at Malta. He writes to his father-in-law, off Toulon, on the 17th of July, 1809, as follows:—

" It gave me great pleasure to find you were enjoying good health, and every happiness that the society of your amiable daughters can give. It is a great blessing, but, I am afraid, one of those which I have little chance

of enjoying. I am pretty well pleased and thankful
when I am not in pain, which, between the head-ache
by day, and cramps by night, is not often the case.
This mortal body of ours is but a crazy sort of machine
at the best of times; and when old, it is always wanting
repair; but I must keep it going as long as I can.
From England they tell me of my being relieved at the
end of the war. I wish to heaven that .the day were
come. But as God wills it."

The last recorded mention of his children by Lord
Collingwood, is in a letter to Mr. Blackett, written on
the 24th of November, 1809. It is as follows:—

"The accounts I receive of my children are my
greatest comfort. God has given them good under-
standings; and if they have imbibed from Mrs. Moss a
proper contempt for vanities and a taste for useful
knowledge, she will have done the duty of a friend for
them, and laid a sure foundation for their happiness.
Their respectability in life, next to their own suavity of
manner to all people, will depend upon a proper selection of their company; such as the flock is, such is the
lamb."

In a similar spirit he writes to Mrs. Hall, the
daughter of his cousin, Admiral Brathwaite, with
whom he first served, on the 7th of October. He
says:—

"I had great pleasure in the receipt of your very
kind letter, a few days since, and give you joy, my dear
Maria, on the increase of your family. You have now
three boys, and I hope they will live to make you very

happy when you are an old woman. I am truly sensible
of the kind regard which you have shown to me in
giving my name to your infant ; he will bring me to
your remembrance often, and then you will think of a
friend who loves you and all your family very much.
With a kind and affectionate husband and three children,
all boys, you are happy, and I hope will ever be so.
But three boys—let me tell you, the chance is very much
against you, unless you are for ever on your guard. The
temper and disposition of most people are formed before
they are seven years old ; and the common cause of bad
ones is the too great indulgence and mistaken fondness
which the affection of a parent finds it difficult to veil,
though the happiness of the child depends upon it. Your
measures must be systematic : when they do wrong,
never omit to reprove them firmly, but with gentleness.
Always speak to them in a style and language rather
superior to their years. Proper words are as easily
learned as improper ones.   And when they do well,
when they deserve commendation, bestow it lavishly.
Let the feelings of your heart flow from your eyes and
tongue ; and they will never forget the effect which
their good behaviour has upon their mother, and this at
an earlier time of life than is generally thought ; for I
consider young children, before they have any reason-
ing faculty, to be guided by a species of instinct. I am
very much interested in their prosperity, and that they
may become good and virtuous men.

  "I am glad that you think my daughters are well-be-
haved girls. I took much pains with them the little time
I was at home. I endeavoured to give them a contempt
for the nonsense and frivolity of fashion, and to establish
in its stead a conduct founded on reason. They could

admire thunder and lightning as any other of God's stupendous works, and walk through a church-yard at midnight without apprehension of meeting anything worse than themselves. I brought them up, not to make griefs of trifles, nor suffer any but what were inevitable.

"I am an unhappy creature, old and worn out. I wish to come to England, but some objection is ever made to it."

The last paragraph found a mournful echo in a letter which he wrote shortly afterwards to the Earl of Northesk, about the dissensions in the fleet. He says :—

"Thornborough is very ill, and is to go home when he can be spared. If I were not a mere stick, I should be ill too; but really I cannot find time to be sick. All those courts-martial give me much pain. How can Englishmen find in their hearts to quarrel with each other, when all their powers are required to defend themselves against the common enemy? It is surely the devil that has got loose amongst mankind. I have not been in port since I left the *Ocean*, and am worn out; whenever I think of England it is with a sigh."

Still his hopes of an engagement with the French fleet were not abandoned; and when the possibility of such an occasion seemed to be more warranted than usual, the old fire would come into his eye, the old vigour seem to infuse his frame; and it is with great spirit and animation that he relates to Lady Collingwood, on the 30th of October, the circumstances of an encounter with the squadron of a French fleet, which was chased on shore by Admiral Martin's division in the Gulf of Lyons.   The serious illness and subsequent death of his old friend, Sir Alexander Ball, former governor of Malta, affected him deeply. "I love him," he said, "and am in despair for him." Amongst the last letters which he wrote is one to his friend, Captain Clavell, which is noticeable for the kindly spirit in which it is written, as well as for the sound advice which it contains.   It is dated from his ship, October 20, 1809 :—

"I am very sorry that you have so little prospect of getting employed at sea; because I am sure that there is no officer who takes the service more to heart, or would do it more justice than you would. I have so little influence at the Admiralty, that I have no reason to suppose anything which I could say would avail you. Lord Mulgrave knows my opinion of you, and the confidence I have in you; but the truth is, that he is so pressed by persons having parliamentary influence, that he cannot find himself at liberty to select those whose nautical skill and gallantry would otherwise present them as proper men for the service.   A hole or two in the skin will not weigh against a vote in Parliament, and my influence is very light at present.   But the French fleet is ready for sea; and if God should bless me with a happy meeting with them, I shall hope that I may afterwards venture to ask a favour, and there is no one for whom I would rather ask it than for you.   In the meantime, occupy yourself in all sorts of naval studies.

Whenever you come forward to service, come with more knowledge than when you left it. It was a misfortune that your health obliged you to go to England; but that was a circumstance not to be avoided. Officers who take the service to heart, as you have always done, will be borne down by the weight of it when it is arduous; and a little relaxation was necessary to you. Except the short time the *Ocean* was under repair at Malta, I have been at sea ever since you left this country. My health and strength are wearing fast away, and I am become an infirm old man; but I am content to be so, and satisfied that my life could be nowhere so well-spent. I am much obliged to you for inquiring about my daughters. I wish you had seen them, for it gives me much pleasure—indeed, it is the only pleasure I have— to hear of them from everybody. It grieves me that Sir Peter Parker is so ill. He is a good man, and has had a parental regard for me. Would that I could rejoice his heart once more with the success of this fleet."

Still in spirits at the prospect of accomplishing a final stroke, Collingwood writes to his father-in-law, hoping the French fleet may come out once more for the purpose of victualling Barcelona, which, at that time, was much in want of provision. But his health was fast failing; during five years he had never left his ship for a single night. Incapacitated as he was by constant confinement, infirmities seized him; he lost all power of digestion; for six weeks he ate almost nothing; his strength fell away, and his last letter was dictated when he could no longer walk across his cabin.

It was evident the end was approaching. His friends had urged him long before to resign his command. Of its necessity he was well convinced, but forbore to do so until he should be relieved in the regular manner. In spite of his sinking health, he never gave way to any alteration in his habits. During his illness, and in the rigours of winter, he never gratified himself with a fire in his cabin, as it was a privilege not allowed to others. How much he would have valued such an indulgence may be inferred from his saying to Mr. Blackwell, some time before, "I do not care about being rich, if we can but keep a good fire in winter." On the 25th of February, 1810, he moored in the harbour of Port Mahon, in the island of Minorca, and was advised by his medical attendant to take a little gentle horse exercise; but it was too late. He was told that the preservation of his life depended on his immediate return to England. With his high respect for discipline it was with great reluctance that he could bring his mind to leave his post, even under these circumstances: but after examining the book of instructions, he resigned his command to Rear-admiral Martin. He felt the hand of death upon him. He knew how cold he might be lying before he should reach England, and ordered a quantity of lead to be shipped at Minorca, to serve for his last enclosure. Two days were occupied in endeavouring to warp the

Ville de Paris out of Port Mahon; on the third a favourable wind came, which wafted him out of the harbour, and sail was made for his own shores—the country which he had loved so well, but was never destined to reach alive. When he was told they were again at sea, his heart revived, and, true to his cause, he exclaimed with satisfaction, "Then I may yet live to meet the French once more." On the morning of the next day—this was the 7th of March—there was a considerable swell on the sea, when his friend, Captain Thomas, came into the cabin, and hoped that it did not disturb him. "No, Thomas," was the reply; "I am now in a state in which nothing can disturb me more. I am dying, and I am sure it must be consolatory to you, and all who love me, to see how comfortably I am coming to my end." The rest may be told in the words of his biographer:—

"He told one of his attendants that he had endeavoured to review, as far as was possible, the actions of his past life, and that he had the happiness to say that his mind was at rest. He spoke at times of his absent family, and of the doubtful contest in which he was about to leave his country involved, but ever with calmness and perfect resignation to the will of God; and in this blessed state of mind, after taking an affectionate farewell of his attendants, he expired, without a struggle, at six o'clock in the evening of that day, having attained the age of fifty-nine years and six months."

" Those who were about his lordship's person," observes Mr. Macanst, the surgeon of the *Ville de Paris*, in the report which he made on the occasion, " and who witnessed the composure and resignation with which he met his fate, will long remember the scene with wonder and admiration. In no part of his lord-ship's brilliant life did his character appear with greater lustre than when he was approaching his end. It was dignified in the extreme. If it be on the bed of sick-ness and at the approach of death—when ambition, the love of glory, and the interests of the world are over —that the true character is to be discovered, surely never did any man's appear to greater advantage than did that of my Lord Collingwood. For my own part, I did not believe it possible that any one on such an occasion could have behaved so nobly. Cruelly harassed by a most afflicting disease, obtaining no relief from the means employed, and perceiving his death to be inevitable, he suffered no sigh of regret or mur-muring at his past life to escape him. He met death as became him, with a composure and fortitude which have seldom been equalled and never surpassed."

Thus passed away the spirit of this great hero. England did not know—perhaps she will never know —what a noble heart she lost on that sad day, how true the pulse within it beat to her welfare and honour, how sound to the core and how rich it was in every good principle which gives value to the name and dignity to the character of an English Christian Gentleman. That the death of so good a man should have been consonant with his life is not a matter of surprise. It was striking in its un-demonstrativeness. He died in the rational and consistent faith in which he had lived. He did not attempt to heighten the mercies of a just God by calling himself hard names. He did not approach the Eternal Father with the cringing demeanour of a slave. He did not charge himself with crimes he had never committed, nor sought to accuse himself where he knew he was innocent : but he carefully reviewed the circumstances of his life, and " was at rest." The good man, the tender husband and father, the undaunted warrior, the fine-spirited patriot; what could he have to accuse himself of? He had spent his life at the post of duty, and foregone all other things for it—the dearest the world could hold for him—all had been given up. Some failings, some weaknesses, some defections no doubt there were : he knew them better than any one else, and showed that he knew them ; but no purpose could have been served by blatant self-accusation and personal depreciation. For, indeed, it is much better, though infinitely more difficult, to endeavour vigorously to remedy what is faulty or wrong during life, than to overwhelm ourselves at the portals of eternity with the fruitless reproaches of unavailing bitterness. Self-recrimination is easy, but self-government and self-correction are difficult: it is much better to apply these than indulge in the former. But what a blessed death is this to die! The raptures of enthusiasm may expire on the lip, transports of mere feeling may exhale as the dew of the morning, the emotion of the heart may fail as the sunshine on an evening cloud; but the foundations of a soul fixed on the solid bases of a noble life spent in the way of duty can never tremble or falter: they are as firm as the universe and one with the Eternal. The souls who can thus live and thus die are as the stars of the firmament, whose blessed lights are beacons to all ages. For their lives the whole world is richer, and their departure from earth is the harvest of heaven.

The body of Lord Collingwood was carried to Gibraltar, and was thence conveyed by the *Nereus* frigate to Sheerness, where it arrived almost as soon as the news of his death. It was there put on board the commissioners' yacht and brought up the Thames to Greenwich. Every ordnance-bearing ship in the river fired twenty-one guns. For three heavy hours the dull reverberation rolled over the city. Several old Greenwich pensioners came to the funeral of their much-loved commander, and were deeply affected at his death. It was also attended by a great concourse of persons of all classes.

In a dark corner of the crypt of St. Paul's, underneath the dome that rears its gilded cross above the roar of busy London, the grave of this good man is to be found. It is a plain flat stone, bearing the simplest inscription. It is in accordance with this world's rule of award that some of its noblest sons should be slighted or forgotten if rumour have failed to cry their merits sufficiently loudly into the popular ear. Why it should be that whilst the mausoleum of the great champion of the Nile lifts itself proudly to the gaze of the stranger, the tomb of one whose deeds were as great, and whose excellences of character were so eminently conspicuous, should be almost hidden from sight and clothed in darkness, is a question only to be answered in remembering the way in which modest merit is too often treated by the popular judgment of mankind, and how little it really seems to care for it. Of all the wondering thousands who visit the Cathedral of the English capital, how many are there who search out the tomb of this great hero, whose deeds, so creditable to his country and honourable to himself, yet speak loudly to those who will listen to them? Of all the unnumbered discourses pronounced from the pulpit over his grave, how many have been framed to direct the attention of the hearers to the grandeur and sweetness which dignified and softened the large nature of this excellent man? How often has his noble disregard of self, his contempt for the world's rewards, his love to God and man furnished a moral for a sermon or an illustration of the better life? It is to be feared not often ; for, indeed, as regards the significance of such splendid examples of high living, modern ecclesiasticism is for the most part entirely dumb and most profoundly indifferent. It loves rather to clothe and entrench itself in creed and dogma and endless speculation, and to point to those as the criterion of the religious state, than to come forth into the world of fact and set up the standard of an assured and fruitful faith, measured by the spirit in which affairs, public and private, are transacted, by the mode in which the more intimate personal and social relationships are conducted and fulfilled, by the practice of a Christian life rather than the acceptance of an ecclesiastical dogma. To the sleeping hero it is no loss that hurrying thousands should go by the place of his burial every day without a thought directed to it. The cool sequestered vale of life had more charms for him than a nation's applause, a nation's honours. A little quietness, a little rest without turmoil or notoriety would have crowned his life with happiness. But to the living it is an infinite loss that his memory should ever be suffered to decay; for such men are very rare: they are the salt of the earth, and confer a dignity on the whole human race. Pilgrims travelled long distances in former days, undergoing the greatest hardships and privations to visit the tomb of a good man or a martyr to religion, either

as an act of devotion, or to get rid of disease, or
to expiate a fault; shall we not find a healing of
many a moral malady, a fresh incentive to duty,
a more elevated view of life in the recollection and
appropriation of the virtues of one so faithful to his
trust, of one who died a martyr, indeed, to his
country, to liberty, in the cause of justice and
honour, for the safety and well-being of the persons
and property of millions?

But although the tomb of the hero is so altogether
unworthy of him, his memorial is preserved in a fine
marble in the church, in the form of a monument
by Westmacott. He lies stretched on a barge,
symbolizing a ship of war, folded in the flags won from
the enemies of his country; a drawn sword clasped
to his breast. Fame extends her arm above him,
whilst Father Thames, with his tributaries, sits
listening to the story of his deeds. However
beautiful this may be as a work of art, one cannot
help feeling that something simpler might better
suit the memory of the man. Not as dead would
one wish to see him; but in a living attitude, as
the warrior against tyranny and usurpation, as the
undaunted defender of his country, as the approved
and uncompromising friend and guardian of liberty;
the eagle eye, the suppressed eagerness, the wiry and
energetic form, triumphing over every difficulty, firm
and unyielding through every kind of danger, sturdy

and immovable in the very face and menace of death.

But perhaps these are matters of small moment in the case of one whose worthiest monument is, after all, not cut in marble, but which occupies a prouder place, and holds a more revered memorial in the hearts and minds of loving men and women. This is the monument which he would most have coveted, and which he best deserved to have—and, indeed, what monument or memorial could any desire better than to have emblazoned the page of history with the noblest deeds; to have been faithful to the trust reposed in him, true to his country, true to his fellow men, true to himself, and true to his Maker?

Lord Collingwood made a just and equitable will, distributing his property amongst the various members of his family, amply providing for Lady Collingwood and his daughters; and having thus, as he said, disposed of the stuff which he left behind him, he prayed God to render the possessors of it contented and happy.

Collingwood is described as having been of a firm and well-knit constitution, spare in person, rather above the middle height, with a full dark eye and an expressive countenance, marking thoughtfulness, decision, and benevolence of character. His habits were extremely temperate; he always ate with an appetite, drank moderately after dinner, but did not indulge in spirits or wine at any other time. His table was furnished well and plentifully, but without display or extravagance. He was marked in attention to his guests, fond of society, lively in manner and disposition, and interspersed his conversation with humorous remarks and anecdotes. He was a good scholar of the old school, remembered his school Latin, could write a French letter, and knew something of the Spanish language. His reading in English literature was varied and extensive. He was dignified in his deportment, calm in his manner and demeanour, and never forgot himself in anger. He seldom left his ship when it could be avoided, and was unremitting in his attention to its good management. A writer quoted in the ' Gentleman's Magazine ' gives the following characteristics of his conduct on shipboard :—

" It was his general rule in tempestuous weather, and upon any hostile emergency that occurred, to sleep upon his sofa in a flannel gown, taking off only his epauletted coat. The writer of this just delineation has seen him upon deck without his hat, and his grey hair floating in the wind, whilst torrents of rain poured down through the shrouds, and his eye, like the eagle's, on the watch. Personal exposure, colds, rheumatism, ague—all seemed nothing to him when his duty called."

That Lord Collingwood was an actual martyr to his country is not to be doubted. He died in his sixtieth year—a ripe, but not an old age. The members of his family were noticeable for the length of years they lived. When Collingwood died, his constitution was perfectly sound, with the exception of the organs of digestion, which had become fearfully impaired and disorganized. If he had been liberated from service at a proper time—at the time when he asked for liberation—there is little doubt that many years would have been added to his life. He was not the less, but the more a hero because he did not die in battle; for he lived to endure and suffer. His life was worn out of him by a much more painful process, bodily and mental, than any which the weapons of an enemy could have brought about. He kept his allegiance true through every vicissitude; and at the latter part of his life, when the anticipation of seeing his loved ones again had altogether vanished, every day was a death. Hope was dead, personal happiness was dead; only the call of duty kept his hand and brain alive. He had already died for his country before physical death laid its hand upon him and bade him resign the mortal tenement.

A life like Collingwood's is worth a thousand sermons and all the religious experience in the world which is no more than experience. He made no profession of honesty—did not satisfy himself with honest resolutions—hardly took the trouble to form them; but lived honestly, and found the name in the fact. He made it his express business to live rightly;

there was no shifting of lines : his bulwarks were
strong, his fortress impregnable.

Perhaps one of the most serious mistakes of the
present time is that we are a good deal more occupied in the reformation of others than in looking
searchingly into our own lives and conduct and re-
forming ourselves.   It is more easy for wealth to
bestow itself to a certain extent in the furtherance
of good objects, than to look closely into the manner
in which it has been accumulated, and to control
its acquisition by the strict rule of conscientious
principle; it is more easy for enthusiasm to vent
itself on the conversion of others, than to make its
own mode of living elevated, pure and noble; it is
more easy to find fault with existing institutions, and
to expose social incompetency, than to oppose to them
the simple obstacle of a large, honest, and disinterested
life.   And yet this is the sole, the only way to be of
any sort of service in regenerating society : to see
clearly and definitely the limits of the circle which
we can touch by a personal and practical exposition
of a right life, and to confine our care and attention
to, and to bring every effort to bear upon observing
that ; leaving all the rest which does not belong to
our function, and which we only cheat ourselves in
attempting to compass, as entirely out of our jurisdiction and responsibility.   In such a life as that of
Collingwood we see this principle exemplified in the

most distinctive manner. He was not a fault-finder; it was not his function to condemn others; he could not alter the moral government of others; to have gone about preaching doctrines of duty in conduct and elevation of life would have been a very vague and uncertain mode of propagating and enforcing them. What he had to do was strictly, thoroughly, and uncompromisingly to fulfil the tasks which had been set before him; to look to his own conduct, his own behaviour; to take care that he himself should think, feel, and act justly and rightly; that he should accept the mission and object of life at their highest significance; that he should discharge all the functions which had been assigned to him in the most complete and thorough manner possible. It thus happened that he did not question himself concerning the failings, negligences, and more positive faults of others, over which he had no power, but gave himself to the scrupulous and exact discharge of his own duties, over which he had an absolute and prevailing control, unmistakable in the efficacy of its exercise, incontrovertible in its results. This he did, therefore: he taught every one by the irresistible weight of practice and example, that a noble life is possible, desirable, and efficacious to all the ends proposed in a just course of human action; that goodness, virtue, and disinterestedness are compatible with the management of the affairs of every day, and may lie

at the heart of an active, energetic, industrious, and
successful life.   He made it clear that to say is
nothing, but to do is much; completing and round-
ing his own destiny in the grand lessons which
he taught to others by maintaining intact the internal rulership of a truth-devoted, earnest, up·
right and reverend spirit, from whose high dictates
he never swerved or faltered.

Collingwood was a deeply religious man; and his
religion is worth dwelling upon for its sterling and
practical genuineness.   That it was sound and of
the right sort is evident, or it could not have produced so noble a life.   It was not composed of in-
terdiction or prescription.   It did not consist in
catering for heaven by the narrow abstinence from
conventionally defined evil, nor sought its own
benefit in the good which it adopted and performed;
but rather to enter into the soul of goodness and
rightness, and to be one with their essence and
spirit.   It was not a mere system of sinning and
repenting, but it consisted of living at the highest
rate possible—always at the best, and forestalling
repentance by a constant attention to duty and strict
watchfulness over self.   It was not satisfied by being
included in a certain religious community or institution holding special tenets or dogmas.   It was not
a religion of set forms and observances.   It did not
place dependence on moods or states of feeling.   It

was all lived.   It was a persistent course of action in doing right, in thinking and feeling justly.   The genuine, solid, and practical character of Collingwood's religion is indicated in a letter which he wrote to Mrs. Moutray, in 1806.   He says,—

"Who would have thought that my orders given for the conduct of a fleet should ever have been preached from a pulpit?   It seems so odd a thing.   God knows it never struck me that there was anything particular in them.   The expressions were merely those that flowed naturally from a heart full of thankfulness to God for the happy issue of a great contest; for, under all our circumstances, it was impossible for any one to consider them, and not to feel a consciousness of divine aid.   The language of the sermon is fine, the doctrine of it highly instructive.   It teaches us where we may safely rest our hope of a happy issue to our endeavours; but not to sit with arms across, crying 'God help us!'   He has given us certain powers, and it is in the exercise of them to the best of our understanding that we may reasonably hope for help."

"He was on every Sunday," says his biographer, Mr. Newnham Collingwood, "a regular and serious attendant at divine worship; and when the state of the weather did not permit the assembling of the crew for that purpose, he was used to retire to his cabin and read the service of the day and some devout book.   His religion was calm and rational, and devoid of all pretence.   It raised his mind naturally upwards in devotion and gratitude towards God, and manifested itself in benevolence towards men."

His religion was like the mainspring of a watch, not exposed to every eye, but indicated distinctly by its results and operations : it was down in the depths of his heart where the sources of his being lay. It was the vehicle of life, and had nothing extraneous or supererogatory about it : it was all brought into use : it was the instigator and ruling agent of all his actions.

Lord Collingwood had little regard for the tangled web of ethical speculation. If he had lived in this age he would probably—nay, very certainly —have been offended and repelled by the fine brain-spinning which constitutes the so-called moral science of to-day. He shamed the passwords of modern philosophies. No system embraced his code, for it was above systems and had a vital energy which systems can never touch. Its only existence was in practice ; it had no being in talk : was not a thing of speculation at all ; but bore its fruits as a tree brings forth its produce, quite naturally ; and then set "budding more." He answered every problem of moral philosophy by removing it from the dark region of speculation into the clear realm of actuality and performance. Every question of political economy was solved in the same manner ; by simply fulfilling his own part completely and effectually in the social machine. Life had no speculative difficulties to him ; every doubt was annihilated in the act of living. Intellectual and spiritual perplexities vanished in the fulfilment of his accepted office and function, in the discharge of the appointed tasks and prescribed obligations of every day.

Of Collingwood's sense of duty as the controlling power of the soul, and his earnestness in fulfilling it, perhaps enough has been said. He loved duty better than life or anything life can give. For every good man the world is better. Each martyr who dies seals a fresh charter of liberty for the race, and ratifies a new franchise for the freedom of souls. All our liberties, rights, and privileges have been fought for and obtained by those who have done their duty. Every earnest and indefatigable worker towards a just end and purpose constitutes a mark or monument in the history of the race. The centuries flow round him, but not over him. Such persons are the large waves which carry the storm, bearing on their bosom all the smaller ones—the dominant billows which throw the tide still higher on the shore. They are the very steps of progress by which elevation is gained, and compensate the sluggishness of tedious and inoperative ages. The debt of the world to these is large; they are the delegates of the Supreme Ruler, and work out the plan of the universe.

There are many proofs, if proof were needed, that

such a destiny is not necessarily confined to great occasions and a large scale of life. The circumstances of every day, the condition of the most insignificant, offer all the materials for its accomplishment. Whoever makes duty his first care need ask no other reward. He has a territory wider than that of kings, and commands treasures more than chancellors. He seeks neither fame nor recompense, if only he have left his race a little better than he found it; if his name be only inscribed on the eternal pillars with the names of those who have not lived in vain. His reward is in his work. It is enough for him that he has finished the task which was prescribed to him, that he can give up his stewardship without any misgiving, any self-reproaches, viewing himself but as the instrument in the hand of a mighty Purpose which has called him from nothingness that its vast ends may be accomplished, its sacred behests completed, its lofty designs fulfilled.

Lord Collingwood was thoroughly English, both by taste and nature. "Of all climates and countries," he says, in one of his letters, " under the sun to live in comfort, there is none like England." It would not have been possible for any other soil or nation to have given birth to such a man. Every country and race has its peculiar order of idiosyncrasy. Lord Collingwood's was entirely and typically that of his own. The heroic elements of his character were without constraint; they were native and easy to him. Probity and frankness were his natural atmosphere: no touch of cunning or duplicity stained the proverbial British candour. He always hung out his colours, and hated the dubious regions of craft and subtlety with a wholesome antipathy. He would abandon a good end rather than use bad means to attain it. He abhorred the name and character of sneak, and before he would follow an underhand course would face a thousand fires. He claimed no privileges from night and darkness, nor would consent that any of his actions, however lawful, should owe anything to disguise or conceal-ment. He had an intense dislike to what is popularly called humbug in every form. When the Spanish prisoners were liberated on their parole, after the battle of Trafalgar, the French had been retained, but when Admiral Rossily applied for permission to transport some of the French wounded to France in a neutral vessel, the request was readily granted on the condition of an exchange of the same number of English prisoners. The provisions of the agreement were, however, not adhered to by Admiral Rossily, who afterwards wrote an apologetic letter to Collingwood, overlaid with ceremonious expressions and complimentary phrases. The value set upon this is indicated by Collingwood having endorsed it, "Admiral Rossily's apology, with some light

Q

French stuff." It was precisely this love of open-
ness and moral daylight which was his safeguard,
his impenetrable armour; which rendered him as
fearless as the wind and as invulnerable; for artifice
is the mother of fear, and doubleness is always in
danger. Entrenched in veracity, his word was his
honour; his promise was as good as his oath; there
was no equivocation with friend or enemy. He had
the right hearty English faith, that success lies in
honesty, and must be reached in no other way. His
lines were straight, and wherever they cut he never
left them. He was a genuine lover of fair play, and
never took a mean advantage. His very reserve was
English, and the desire not to make too much of
himself or his impressions. He disliked noise and
vapour. Such reticence of words perhaps never
existed before in company with so many glorious
actions. His flag wore no motto but that which was
woven in the material of substantial deeds. Whatever he did he left his hand upon it, and that was
its history and the whole tale of it.

In Collingwood were united the extremes of
strength and tenderness. A lion in defence of
his country, or as the combatant of usurpation
and tyranny, at home he was the good husband and
affectionate father. Peace was his element, though
he was forced to war. Though called to strife and
turmoil, and charged with the burdensome office of

the most difficult diplomacy, his more desired function was the fulfilment of the social and domestic
round, the cultivation of his garden, dressing his
oaks or hoeing his cabbages with old Scott. The
education of his children, a certain philosophic ease,
cheap pleasures and country delights were dearer to
him than the honour of statesmanship or the glories
of war.

Other of his traits specially English were the
distinctively serious view he took of the business
part of his profession, and his punctuality in the
discharge of it. All his conduct and transactions
were ruled by the genii of method and order. The
smallest matter of business or circumstance connected
with his profession received the fullest and most
careful acquittance. It was never taken by the way,
trifled with, or mixed up with recreation or relaxation. Everything connected with his office was
paramount, express, and obligatory, admitting no
slightness, neglect, delay, or procrastination. Nor
was one thing thought of less importance than
another. The least must be despatched with the
greatest; the whole round must be completed. For
just as Nature in all her works never forgets the last
touch, so he who would live the perfect life must
not leave anything undone: a right consummation
allows no slurring or negligence.

Collingwood was a staunch Conservative, though

not an ignorant or prejudiced one. His social and
political faith was broad; for it was founded on the
basis of a real humanity, and not upon the clouds
of an airy fantasy and insubstantial speculation.
But with every liberality of feeling, he inclined to
the old rather than the new. A friend to existing institutions, he looked upon innovations with
suspicion, and gave himself to administer the old
systems perfectly rather than to quarrel with them
and clamour for new ones. When at Morpeth, in
1792, and the revolutionary spirit of France began
to show itself in certain classes in England, he says,
in a letter to Nelson, "Misery will undoubtedly be
the consequence of any commotion or attempt to
disturb our present most excellent constitution."
He recognised the fact, laid small stress upon by
political economists, writers of voluminous tomes,
and lovers of long speeches, that every reform—the
only effectual reform—begins with the individual,
and is comprised in the fulfilment of personal duty;
for this supersedes acts of parliament and lightens
the labour of legislation. He understood and recognised the truth, that robust and conscientious men
and women make a nation great, and that national
greatness can be reached in no other way than
by the elevation of individual character. Collingwood was proud of the institutions of his country,
though he did not fail to protest against their

abuses. He accepted them, as he did his ship; he wasted no time in wishing for better than he sailed in, and, instead of depreciating it, sought to make himself its perfect master, and to get the best possible service out of it. " I have too much reverence for the law," he writes to Mr. Grenville, " to violate it intentionally. I have ever, to the best of my understanding, made it my guide, and the temperate administration of it my study." He disliked demagogy and the loquacity of noisy controversialists. He writes to Mr. Blackett, in 1796 :—

" The tumultuous associations and clubs in England, and the license they have taken in their acts and publications, afflict me. Some attach themselves to violent parties from an unhappy disposition, delighting in whatever is turbulent; some from fashion; and very many from folly, being entirely incapable of judging of the propriety of the measures which they censure."

His notions of government scarcely admitted revolution, for the reason that his administration needed none. For, indeed, there is something better than revolutions and reformations : it is the condition which does not require them. To such men as Collingwood the act makes the law, and the law is good because the act is right.

We see in Collingwood the model of a Christian Gentleman. His nature included all that is implied by the term "breeding" in its highest sense and application. His good manners were without monkey-ism, conventionality or affectation. They had nothing of the assumption or insincerity of a Chester-field, or the fantastic apishness of a Brummell. They were a part of his large heart, the offspring of good feeling, tact, correct judgment, and sympathetic consideration. They were not reserved for certain persons or classes, but were distributed upon all with whom he came into contact. His behaviour was always dignified and in good taste. He never ex-hibited violence of manner; his voice was calm, his words few and weighty, and so firm in command, that they were feared by neglect and defalcation more than blows. His courtesy was unexceptional. It was remarked that the youngest and least distinguished guest at his table received the same measure of attention as the most illustrious. Although the foundation of his good manners lay deeper, he would not be outdone in an act of politeness. When the governor of Syracuse met him on the beach with his coach and six horses, the former, as a mark of respect, mounted the driving-seat, and sat beside the coachman, in order that Collingwood might occupy the body of the carriage alone; upon which Colling-wood at once got out, and failing to persuade the governor to take his seat in the carriage, he bade the postilion dismount, saying that if his master took the coachman's place he would drive the leaders, and was positively mounting one of the horses in his full-dress uniform, when a compromise was effected, and both occupied their places in the carriage. He had none of the snobbishness of the upstart, nor any of the no less offensive pretentiousness, intolerance, and arrogance which sometimes make established rank and position insufferable. "Poor fool!" he says of a dishonest trickster, "not to know how much respect is due to a virtuous man, though poor, and how much contempt to a wealthy knave." As has been already stated, he would not allow his sailors to be addressed excepting in terms of civility. He had no official bustle and fussiness. He did not seek to magnify his office, or to use it as the instrument of display, or for the purpose of adding to his personal importance. He had none of the quality of which "red tape" has been used as the symbol, allowing official rule and regulation to impede what they were intended to facilitate, or to stand in the way of the course of action to be pursued. "Cultivate his esteem," he says, in writing to Captain Clavell of a brother captain; "he has a great deal of enterprise, and can step out of the beaten path to do a good thing." Thackeray, in his lectures upon the 'Four Georges,' pays a high tribute to the chivalric character of Collingwood. He says,—

"Another true knight of those days was Cuthbert

Collingwood, and I think, since heaven made gentlemen, there is no record of a better one than that. Of
brighter deeds, I grant you, we may read performed by
others; but where of a nobler, kinder, more beautiful
life of duty, of a gentler truer heart? Beyond dazzle
of success and blaze of genius, I fancy shining a hundred
and a hundred times higher the sublime purity of
Collingwood's gentle glory. His heroism stirs British
hearts when we recall it. His love, and goodness, and
piety make one thrill with happy emotion. As one
reads of him and his great comrade going into the
victory with which their names are immortally connected, how the old English word comes up, and that
old English feeling of what I should like to call
Christian honour."

Admirable as is this testimony to the worth of a
good man, it must, nevertheless, be allowed to be imperfect in one respect. Thackeray could hardly have
studied Collingwood's life or the history of his doings
thoroughly, or he would surely have added another
leaf to his laurels, another jewel to his crown. Upon
my word, I do not know in all the narrative of
bright deeds any more distinguished or more notably
and distinctly important than those of Lord Collingwood with Lord Howe in 1794, at St. Vincent and
at Trafalgar, as well as on other occasions. I do not
know who has done more brilliant deeds with more
peril to himself; who has exhibited more daring,
more energy and ability with more momentous

results than did Lord Collingwood, or who has said less about them. I do not think that, even as actions, apart from the character of the man, his brave deeds have ever been surpassed, anywhere or at any time. It is true his unobtrusive disposition and the want of a certain popular element in his character may have prevented them from obtaining their merited weight in general estimation, but that does not detract from their essential importance and real nobleness. In scope of mind and far-seeing sagacity he has rarely been equalled ; nor must the possession of a high order of cultivated genius be denied to him. As a matter of fact, Trafalgar may be said to have been won by Collingwood just as much as by Nelson, and he took as active a part in it. Collingwood's claims to be numbered amongst the heroes of England are first-rate, not second-rate.

One of the brightest jewels in his character was his patriotism. It was, indeed, of the grandest order. It did not consist in high-sounding phrases. It was like the fire upon sacred altars, lighted at the sun and kept perpetually burning. It was a genuine emotion as well as a comprehensive principle, and had the intrinsic power over him of a close and personal relationship. It was a component of his nature, and not an assumed panoply. He always bore it with him, for it was a part of him. He served his country, not by wishing it well, but by doing well

for it; by being faithful to its welfare, true to its best
interests, and indefatigable in promoting them. "I
am sorry," he says, "so active an officer as Colonel
—— should not be employed; what should I suffer,
if, in this convulsion of nations, this general call of
Englishman to the standard of their country, I should
be without occupation?—a miserable creature! While
it is England, let me keep my place in the front of
the battle." The burden of his country's sorrows
and perils weighed upon him much more heavily
than his own. "In bodily strength," he says in one
of his letters, "I am worn out; and whoever enters
so entirely into the state of our country as I do, and
have done, cannot be much otherwise." "Alas, poor
England!" he exclaims, seeing the dangers with
which she was threatened; "Heaven knows but we
may yet live to mourn over its grave." "My only
object in this world," he says, in a letter to Lord
Radstock, "is the interest of my country; and if I
go wrong in my endeavours to maintain it, the error
will be in my judgment, and not in my heart."
All these professions of devotion to his country would
be of little value, if they were not rendered
absolutely insignificant when compared with his
large acts and conscientious conduct. With such
champions as these to call her own, the Genius of our
islands may well grasp her trident with a firmer
hand and wear her casque with a finer air, proud of

her sons and of the place which they occupy in the
history of nations.

A prominent feature in Lord Collingwood's character was his strong self-reliance. He leaned upon
his own powers of determination as upon the
buttresses of a rock, and they did not fail him. His
purposes were written upon adamant and were in-
effaceable. His resolution stood in the midst of the
sea of opinion and the fluctuations of circumstance
like a pharos, a watch-tower. The storm might
beat upon it, the tempest might arise and lash the
roaring foam into frenzied rebellion; but untouched
by the anger of wind and wave, unshaken by the
turbulence that reigned around, it raised itself above
the disorders of the elements and the confused forces
of the world, safe upon the security of its own
immovable foundations. Of what a royal demesne,
indeed, is he the ruler who holds firmly the reins of
self-government! Of what wealth-bearing seas is he
the master who grasps with a strong hand the helm
of an undeviating resolution and self-control, and
knows the end of his voyage where the havens of
rest lie, suffering no object or distraction to divert
him from the strict line of his course! What an
epoch is that to the individual who has been ac-
customed to surrender himself to the sway of events,
passion, interest, or the will of others, when he first
assumes the command of his own soul, the direction

of his own life! What a new world he enters! What
an amazing power does he find to reside within himself! Of what a strength of endurance and resistance
in adversity does he find himself capable! what
coolness and equanimity in prosperity are within his
reach! Let a man once learn to separate his course
of action from his immediate and exclusive interests,
to guide himself by the directions of reason, and not
be driven hither and thither by accident, opinion, or
the desire of self-gratification—and what a splendid
dawn suffuses his soul! How glorious the mastery,
the dominion which he holds! How do the billows
subside on the darkened sea of life, hushing their
portentous mutterings and despairing murmurs as the
hurricanes of impulse and passion are stayed and
the world's wild race ceases to whirl the soul in its
giddy vortices, and the heavens are broken up, and
the stars of hope come forth to light the path which
leads to the land of his desired rest, the grand end
of a purpose fulfilled, a destiny accomplished, the
crown of completed duty won! But not at once can
he reach the much-desired region; for just as the
muscles of the body are strengthened by use, so the
powers of a rigorous and unyielding resolution are
only attained by prolonged effort, and can only be
strengthened by persistent exercise, until, like well
tempered steel, they cannot be broken.

It is astonishing what an engine of power a single

individual may become who has once learnt to know the full weight and value of his own will, and what a stupendous instrument it may be made in the hands of an implicit self-reliance based upon its tried strength and approved service. Unswayed by either fortune, it ploughs its way like a vessel through the trackless expanse of the ocean, itself making the path which it pursues. To be able to avert or avoid the evils which threaten us, or to disarm them when they come upon us, to rely upon our resolutions as upon inviolable laws, to find our highest good in ourselves, and to open the inexhaustible fountains of spiritual strength by applying to the inward sources of energy and self-dependence, are to be numbered amongst the most eminent acquirements and most precious privileges of humanity: and those who help to reveal to us the means and organs of the powers which are at our command, and who point out a more extended use of them, confer upon us the boon of an inheritance whose value is beyond the calculations of arithmetic to discover or the dreams of the imagination to conceive. Perhaps there is no more grand or useful attainment possible to the soul than, without selfishness, moroseness, or indifferent sympathies, to be able to stand alone, to ask the help of no living arm when the battle is thickest and closest; but to carve a way through every obstacle, by whatever difficulties we may be

surrounded. It is only to a manly independence of
feeling that the highest kind of affection and friendship is possible. It is only he whose mind is
perfectly staid upon itself who can either offer or
afford support to others. The sympathy of the
spiritually weak is of little service compared with
that of the strong. Those who have never suffered
bravely are poorly fitted to support or console others
under affliction, or to bestow a peace in exigences in
which they themselves have failed to find it. In
Collingwood we see united the warmest sympathy
with the firmest self-reliance. He not only knew
how to bestow sympathy, but to suggest a remedy,
and help with his advice. Yet, with all his self-
reliance, he was not in the least degree obstinate.
He could give way gracefully to the wishes of others
where there was a favour to be bestowed or a
pleasure to be conferred ; but such a sacrifice of his
own desires and intentions to the will of others only
served to strengthen his own in the exercise of the
self-denial which made the concession.

Intimately connected with this quality in Lord
Collingwood's character was that of an unfailing
presence of mind. He was never taken by surprise
or disconcerted by events, however unexpected.
When in the Mediterranean, on the *Excellent,* in
1796, one of the vessels, the *Princess Royal,* on a
dark and rainy night, ran on board his ship. With

the utmost readiness he sheered off his own vessel, escaping with the loss of a bowsprit and fore-mast, when a moment's delay or hesitation would probably have been fatal to his ship and all on board. Indeed, however much he might be harassed or disturbed, it was observed that occurrences of difficulty or danger had the immediate effect of dispelling every sort of anxiety from his mind, producing the utmost coolness of mood and behaviour. Smith, his attendant, says,

" The admiral spoke to me about the middle of the action of Trafalgar, and again for five minutes immediately after its close; and on neither occasion could I observe the slightest change from his ordinary manner. This, at the moment, made an impression on me which will never be effaced; for I wondered how a person whose mind was occupied by such a variety of most important concerns, could, with the utmost ease and equanimity, inquire kindly after my welfare, and talk of common matters as if nothing of any consequence were taking place."

This power of summoning up courage for every occasion is referable to the fact that Collingwood's bravery was not an animal instinct, or the mere impulse of an impetuous nature; it was not the result of a love of excitement, the desire for adventure, or for the opportunity to display a gallant spirit; neither was it the blindness of temerity which fears no danger but what it is made to feel and suffer; it was not compounded of recklessness or thoughtlessness. It was courage disciplined by reason. It was the settled purpose and determined resolve of one who hated bloodshed and slaughter to quell the enemies of his country; and for this he set aside all his personal predilections, all the repugnance of his nature to the work he had to do, and addressed himself to his task by crushing every feeling that rebelled against it. In the spirit of true bravery he counted the cost and accepted the sacrifice. For, indeed,—

"The brave man is not he who feels no fear,
  For that were foolish and irrational;
  But he whose noble soul that fear subdues,
  And bravely dares the danger nature shrinks from."

It was this power of self-command which enabled him to meet every exigency with boldness and to triumph over all opposition, invincible in the confidence of the justice of his cause and unconquerable in the temper which he brought to further it. Of the value of his courage and the proofs of it, his brave deeds already narrated are the sufficiently abundant guarantees, though the narrative is doubtless an incomplete one.

Lord Collingwood was ruled by a strong principle of order. There was no confusion or irregularity in his brain or his work. So methodical was he in all he did, and so precise in exacting the same observance

of system in others that when he saw any failure
in this respect he frequently spoke with some degree
of asperity and a certain hastiness of manner
which were constitutional with him; and although
on these occasions he never forgot himself or the
dignity which belonged to his nature and character,
and was never betrayed into improper or violent
language, yet there is no doubt that where he was
not fully known they often conveyed a false or
imperfect opinion of his real character. He would
have been altogether more than human if he had
been able to preserve the uncompromising standard
which he held before himself with absolute mildness
of manner and demeanour amongst the untoward
and frequently rebellious elements which he had to
keep in serviceable order by the rules of a strict
and efficient organisation. Indeed, it would have
been impossible to have done so. Neither would it
have been possible for any one in the constant
exercise of so many and so great self-denials, only
to be maintained at the expense of much internal
warfare, and suffering at the same time from a
depressed nervous system and impaired bodily health,
to have taken part in the events passing around him
with a mood at all times equalized and unruffled. The
quickness of temperament, however, thus indicated
was only superficial, and was never misunderstood by
those to whom he was well known. It never had

R

any hold upon or foundation in his profounder nature; for, whenever the finer and higher principles of his character were appealed to, they were never found wanting. External irritants might ruffle the surface, but beneath them lay the calm, grand elements of a consolidated spiritual being which they never penetrated, whose beams were stedfastly fixed upon the assured foundations of a reasonable and benevolent nature.

Lord Collingwood was distinguished by great liberality and generosity of disposition, and the entire absence of avarice or narrowness of mind in regard to this world's goods. He refused to admit the desire for wealth or the struggle to obtain it as a ruling principle in the economy of his life. He valued wealth at its true worth; as to a certain extent a useful addition to the nobler treasures of the soul, but a cumbersome and useless impediment when accepted as an absorbing and exclusive object where the latter did not hold an infinitely higher place, or where they were altogether superseded or disregarded. No amount of wealth could induce him to compromise for a moment the least of his principles in order to obtain it. He writes to Mr. Blackett about his newly bequeathed property :—

"I never can care enough about Chirton to consider much about it. One thing only interests me—that no person should be removed from a house or farm unless his conduct has made him very obnoxious. It is the interest of an old tenant to give a fair rent; and when he does, it is shameful to have him subjected to a higher bidder. I have lived now long enough without wealth to be indifferent about it; and I hope I may always be comfortable without putting others to difficulty."

"Let others solicit pensions," he says; "I am an Englishman, and will never ask for money as a favour." "If I had a favour to ask," he says in another place, "money would be the last thing I would beg from an impoverished country. I have motives for my conduct which I would not give in exchange for a hundred pensions." Wherever he saw an avaricious or mercenary spirit in the service, he never failed to speak of it with marked disapprobation and contempt as derogatory to the profession. "I had hoped," he writes to Captain Clavell, "that your long cruise in the Adriatic would have turned out more profitable to you than it has done; but I trust you will always look upon that as quite a secondary consideration." He anticipated the formal order for a cessation of hostilities with Spain at the commencement of the revolution in that country by urging the Spanish Junta to prevent the sailing of their vessels, which he heard were about to run from the Canary Islands, though, if they had been allowed to do so, they might have become lawfully his prize—no doubt a very valuable one.

R 2

Lord Collingwood had learned the happy art of contentment.   He did not trouble himself by wishing for what he had not got, but rather to make the most of that which he had.   He neither sought the smiles nor avoided the frowns of fortune; but to do justly and live nobly, regarding all the rest with indifference.   A stain upon his soul would have turned a world of gold to a heap of ashes and poisoned all its uses.   All he asked was an untarnished honour, the sweet possession of an uncorrupted life, a mind undisturbed by the clamours of the multitude, and the treasures of an upright and conscientious spirit.   Sober desires, chastened and temperate wishes, superseded the hot and feverish struggles of ambition and greed; the gilded pageants of time lost their lustre to a sight so true, fading, like stars at dawn, before aims so elevated and a conduct so splendid and magnanimous.

His mercy and humanity have been already illustrated: the prisoners of the enemy were always cared for in the fullest manner possible.   His object was to avoid and prevent all unnecessary suffering. When off the Dardanelles in 1807 he issued an order to the fleet, that if any ships of the enemy should take fire or be in extreme distress, no brigs, tenders, or boats occupied in saving the crews of such ships must be fired upon or interrupted in the duty.   His commiseration for affliction or want was always ready.

His acts of charity were numerous; and it is said that he was never known to reject the petition of real distress.

He was perfectly unselfish, and entirely without any littleness of feeling or personal jealousies. He exhibited no trace of a grudging or an envious spirit. He knew that a large and faithful life carried its own credentials and superseded every reputation. He stood upon his acts, his practice, not upon the opinion which might be formed of them : those were his, but this he could not rule and did not value. His praise was always ready for merit, and was never restrained or stinted. He never failed to recommend the best and most deserving officers, deploring the neglect of their merits more than indifference to his own. In the middle of June, 1809, when he was himself suffering the extremities of fatigue from overwork, and the shadow of death lay already upon him, he wrote to the Earl of Mulgrave :—

"Admiral Thornborough has for some time past been falling into an ill state of health, and, I am much afraid, must apply to your Lordship for relief. The state of Captain Bennet and Captain Inglis alarms me very much. Lord Henry Paulett received material injury from a fall which he had in a gale of wind; he does not complain, but it is obvious that his general health has suffered greatly. I mention these circumstances, because I am sure your Lordship will regard the condition of those officers as much as is consistent with the public service."

Another letter of his is so full of a hearty pleasure in the welfare of two of his officers whom he knew to be deserving that I cannot resist transcribing it. It is written to Captain Thomas from the *Dreadnought*, in Cawsand Bay, on the 15th of December, 1804:—

"I find the *Amphion* is to sail in a few days for the Mediterranean, and just write a line to ask you how you do, how you like your ship, and to send you my best wishes for your success and welfare. Everything that happens good to you will give me pleasure. I have only to hope that you may come into some active service, when your zeal and skill may be known; and I have no doubt that in good time they will be rewarded. All your old shipmates who are now with me are well; Clavell, a pattern of industry, gives me great satisfaction, and nothing I more wish than to have it in my power to do him a service. I have been in the *Dreadnought* four or five months past; she does not sail well, but is in other respects a fine ship. Give my kind love and regards to Lord Nelson when you see him."

A review of the characteristics of Lord Collingwood would be hardly complete without noting the beauty and elegance of his literary style. There is nothing strained or feverish about it. It is easy, lucid, harmonious, and unaffected. It was the reflection of his own character and the natural language of his heart tempered and elaborated by a careful study of the best models. What is true of his private correspondence is true also of his official despatches. "I know not where Lord Collingwood got his style," said an eminent English diplomatist with whom he corresponded, "but he writes better than any of us." Of Collingwood's powers of diplomatic correspondence few examples have been given in this volume, as it would require long extracts to furnish a complete idea of the tact, temperance, and clear judgment which distinguished this part of his function. Nothing is more remarkable than its flexibility and versatility. In his correspondence with the Eastern powers his letters read almost like translations from their own tongue; and yet they are quite easy and natural, almost familiar, in composition. A perusal of the most purely official and technical of his orders and despatches relating to the business part of the affairs of the fleet give evidence of extraordinary care, foresight, and attention to the smallest minutiæ, expressed in language at once terse, perspicuous, and pointed.

Every good man makes a good life more practicable; he opens the way to still higher regions of moral elevation, and brings the apparently unattainable within reach. He instils confidence into diffidence, bestows courage upon timidity, and translates unsubstantial doubt into tangible certainty; he gives truth to speculation, sight to faith, consistency to supposition, possession to anticipation, and exchanges the stagnant and stifling atmosphere of spiritual bondage and imprisonment for the wholesome air of an enfranchised liberty. Collingwood left no talent unused. He lived at the top of his powers. He neither wasted nor neglected anything which he possessed. His perseverance and energy were inexhaustible. "I would rather die anyhow," he says, "than with grief and disappointment." He preached England the fine homily of a good example. He made fast friends with the angel of a virtuous life. He espoused Rectitude in unfaltering allegiance, and never left her. In the line of his life-course we see the keen eagle flight which makes straight for the sun. Such men gild the centuries and fill the world with a good odour. Their birth is an epoch. They honour and dignify their race and country. Like Prometheus of old, they bring down fire from heaven and diffuse a hopeful warmth through the hearts and lives of men. They are the electric strings which join earth to heaven. They borrow their light and motion from the courses of the planets, and symbolize the order and glory which are unchangeable. With what a ravishing sense of moral beauty is the mind filled as we direct our mental gaze to a life like this—processional, regular, embodying the great principles of the heavenly law! The excellency of the marble ideal of Greece, the spiritual glow and fulness of the Italian picture, the elevation of the noblest strains of music, the softest song of the sweetest bird, the delight of well-kept gardens, the beauty of the fairest earthly forms, of the flower, of the cloud, the varied landscape—all seem blended and interwoven into the nature of a beautiful soul, of which, indeed, they are only the imperfect types and symbols; for, of all kinds of beauty, moral beauty is the most admirable, the most lovely.   No sensation can equal the thrill of sublime pleasure which flashes through the mind as it contemplates the order and being of a virtuous soul unenthralled by sense, unswayed by passion, freed from selfishness, indifferent to opinion, maintaining the sovereignty of a grander cast of principles than those which are common to the world; which reads its laws on the imperishable scroll, invisible to the slaves of time and of mortal things; whose penetrative vision outreaches the limits of the universe, and rests upon those constellated tablets on which are written the will and purposes of the Eternal.

Such lives as that of Collingwood teach us never to rest satisfied with less than the best, to select our highest moods and most splendid moments, and then to draw up our lives to the same distinguished level. They reveal to us the great possibilities which we possess, the exalted condition which it is within our power to reach.   By such examples the soul is

wakened to a newer and more expansive life. It
passes into a region where there is no doubt, no
perplexing speculations, no groaning beneath the
burden of unfulfilled duties, no self-dissatisfaction,
no groping, no darkness.   It is light as the pathway
of angels, as clear and defined as the galaxy of an
unclouded midnight, coursing from heaven to heaven,
strewing its way with a thousand glories.   For
indeed there is no paradise on earth, no substantial
happiness or satisfaction, where our highest relationships are ignored or disregarded, where an exactly true
and just course of living is held secondary to any other
object, either in theory or practice.   Nothing else
but an uncompromising adherence to substantial
right will serve to calm the soul, to lift it into the
pure realms of peace and contentment, and to place
it out of the reach of earthly powers to disturb or
annoy.

Such men as Collingwood have nothing prospective,
supposititious, or presumptive about them.   They
justify their credentials, and may be measured by
the standard which they set up.   They leave nothing
to credit or trust, but are their own security and
discharge.   Their promise is less than their performance.   Their time of action is always the present ;
they do not thrust their burdens upon the next hour,
nor conserve themselves for great opportunities and
the crises of extraordinary occasions.   They mould

every moment to their wishes : their motto is, Now is the time. It is only thus that the business of a great life is completed ; only by seizing every instant and every circumstance that the whole man is transformed into an image of power and arrives at the heroic height. Each moment and every act reflect a lifetime and the sum total of character. Life is like a mirror with a thousand facets—however small they may be, we see ourselves in every one of them.

Collingwood translated the high commands of duty into a language which all can understand. The confused elements of the universe became in his hands the orderly exponents of great facts. He superseded the unproductive formalism of speculative dogma, and effectually resolved the enigmas of scholastic philosophies, by the most direct and substantial of processes : he tried them by their uses ; the grain was gathered and the chaff driven to the winds by one and the same means. The test was an unfailing one ; they were either tangible and useful for the purpose of living, and on this account worthy of acceptance and appropriation, or else they were a stumbling block and an incumbrance, and to be ruthlessly rejected or disregarded, however venerable and authoritative.

We do not read in the histories of either ancient or modern times of a heroism more splendid, of a disinterestedness more sublime ; or of any who

maintained more inviolably the sanctities of an uncorrupted honour, who exemplified more conspicuously the sovereign excellencies of unstained truth.
Perhaps never were so warm a heart and so affectionate a nature combined with so much manly energy
and uncompromising dignity of principle; so much
prudence, tact, and forbearance, with so undaunted
a spirit; so indomitable a bravery and masculine
decision of character with so much tenderness and
sweetness of disposition; so many graceful traits
within lines so firm, subsisting in so amicable a relationship.   Indeed, it is this multitudinousness of
character, this rare union of so many great qualities,
which constitutes Collingwood's chief distinction.
Singly, they are not unique.   For, however seldom
characters so well balanced, of so complete and
rounded an organization, may be found amongst us,
happily there are always those whose best efforts are
given to the fulfilment of duty, who uphold the
English name in maintaining a high and honourable
spirit in all their undertakings, who devote themselves
to their work without calculating on the reward, who
are content to serve a great principle instead of an
individual and selfish advantage.   Of these the
greater proportion will always remain unnamed
beyond the circle of their operations.   The man of
the age will be continually eclipsed by the man of
the hour.   But if the laws of his conduct be fixed on

a right basis, this will never cause him a moment's
pain or dissatisfaction; for indeed it is not he who
is the loser, but rather those who choose to look with
indifference upon the principles by which he is
governed, and to disregard the example afforded by
his work. The conscientious worker in a just cause
will be quite content to be personally ignored so that
his work prosper, his ends be accomplished, and the
principles he advocates and inculcates be taken up
and carried forward. Perhaps, indeed, there is no
more unfailing test of our sincerity and disinterestedness in what we do than to inquire whether we wish
ourselves to be distinguished, or our work to be
furthered—to ascertain if we would be content that
our trust should be fulfilled, that our actions should
speak—whilst our names and personalities are overlooked or forgotten. If a column could be erected to
the world's nameless heroes of an altitude propor-
tioned to their deserts, with what a surpassing height
would it overtop the glories of existing monuments!
and if the inscription upon it could be made adequate
to their merits, how greatly would it transcend all
the terms of recorded human praise! If it is kingly
to do a noble act and get no thanks for it, what shall
we say of those who are content to leave an anonymous
benefit to society unacknowledged and unrewarded,
excepting by the use which is made of it and the
service to which it is put? For such as these the

race of man is called only a little lower than the angels, and holds the title-deed of its relationship to the Divine.

To such honours let every one who is ambitious of the eminences of a noble life subscribe; and not only so, but enlist himself well in their service, sealing the deeds of so good a precedent with the corroboration of his own. To live in the glories of our ancestors and upon the praise of our heroes is the easy compromise of idleness or indifference; but the energetic seeker after good will not be content with admiring ' their great deeds. He will strive to emulate them in all the courses of a noble ambition, and a life pitched to the same high standard. To the lofty principles which govern the conduct of such men as Lord Collingwood we may give our whole suffrages with the most unreserved confidence, as being absolutely inviolable and perfectly efficacious. Whilst the shifting forms of ecclesiastical systems keep changing from time to time; whilst creeds are contested and dogmas fought for and won and lost, here is something which never changes; here is something upon which may be laid the basis of all that makes human life dignified and honourable—a rock which will never give way, a fortress for the soul which is impregnable. About the necessity for, and value of, an earnest and upright life in all our affairs, thoughts, and actions, there can be no manner of doubt. Its value is never depreciated. Its elements never change. They were the same two thousand or ten thousand years ago as they are now. Time cannot alter or lessen their importance in the least degree. It is these which should command our most jealous care; it is these which should hold a ruling force over us; it is these which should be the end and aim of our existence. They admit no compromise, they allow no substitute; they are absolute and indisputable. Whatever other new things we adopt or old things abandon, we may rest assured that the only thing of essential consequence is the regulation of our lives by the noblest standard, the attainment of the highest possible condition of persistent moral purity and earnestness. All religion and moral science which do not directly, immediately, as their first, last, and sole object, conduce to and consist in these, we may safely leave to the portion of those who prefer husks and refuse to the solid and substantial viands of the sacred feast, to which we have all received the Divine bidding, by means of which alone we enter the ranks of the really great and good. For the attainment of so eminent a situation, it is necessary to keep well before us, enshrined in the soul's innermost chambers, the splendid example of those heroic spirits who have struggled through the clouds which hide the heavenly summits and shown us the way; to measure our course by the great principles by which they were governed; to find the path through darkness up to light, and to be brave and true as they were. These are the great leaders in the battle of life, the generals who know how to marshal their forces, and to meet the enemy in an invincible spirit. With such examples before us, we may do much. Under such leadership, Christianity will assume a more sterling and vital importance, a grander because a more practical significance than any which it is the fashion of the day to assign to it. Emancipated from the burdensome shackles and trammels of speculative generations, we shall meet the Great Captain and Example of all that a good and noble life ought to be face to face, clear in the fulness of that spiritual light by means of which we discern that rectitude and goodness have an intrinsic value far, far above anything to which they can lead us, or anything which they can bestow upon us, lovely and precious in and for themselves alone, and beggaring every other kind of wealth and happiness.

APPENDIX.

IN some recently published letters of Admiral Sir
Edward Codrington* several rather severe stric-
tures are made on the character and conduct of Lord
Collingwood, which seem to me to be based on that
misconception or misunderstanding which so frequently
arises between natures and characters essentially different. Admiral Codrington's first charge against Lord
Collingwood, when off Cadiz, 4th September, 1805
(Admiral Codrington being at this time captain of the
Orion), is that he is "a stay-on-board admiral, who
never communicates with anybody but upon service."
As the anxiety of his duty at that responsible time and
the necessity for the very strictest vigilance have been
already rendered apparent, one may well understand
that Collingwood at such a moment would not only
confine himself as closely as possible to his own ship,
but desire that every other commander should do the
same.

He says that on Sunday morning before the battle of

* 'Memoir of the Life of Admiral Sir Edward Codrington, with
selections from his public and private correspondence.' Edited by
his daughter, Lady Bourchier, 1873.

S

Trafalgar Lord Nelson, " as a compliment to Collingwood," called him on board the *Victory* by signal to
consult with him, with the predetermination to take
no advice which did not correspond with his own
opinion.   A proceeding very unlike Nelson who, in
deputing Collingwood second in command of the
fleet, and from his general conduct towards him, must
certainly have had some sort of confidence in his
judgment.   If Admiral Codrington was correctly informed that Nelson made such an observation, it must
have been a jest, and could never have been intended
as a slight on Collingwood's character or ability.

He complains that after the battle of Trafalgar
Lord Collingwood allowed him no opportunity of
communicating with his friends as to his welfare or
otherwise.   When he next sees Collingwood he learns
something which ought for ever to have silenced his
charge of want of consideration in his commander;
namely, that an account of his safety had been transmitted by the first schooner which left for England
after the battle.   Admiral Codrington ill-naturedly
adds, " but perhaps it was only that I was not otherwise reported to him "; though it is not likely
that Lord Collingwood would have made· a statement of this kind unless he had been certain of
its truth.   He then blames him for not coming to
anchor immediately after the battle.   This question
has already been considered with very different conclusions by those who are much better able to form
a judgment upon it than I.   If a landsman may
be allowed to hold any opinion at all on such a
subject from a common-sense point of view, it would
appear not only undesirable for any ship capable of

making headway to anchor on the lee shore of an
enemy in the face of a hurricane, with defective
anchors, cables, and rigging, but absolute madness to
do so. Indeed, when the command was given, few ships
were able to anchor, in consequence of the damage
which the gear had sustained. On this question, however, I must refer my readers to authorities with whom
the subject has been more ably discussed. Admiral
Codrington also accuses Collingwood of dilatoriness in
the disposal of the fleet after the battle, though we
know he was closely occupied in surveying for report
and draughting off the most disabled vessels. Reflec-
tions on the seamanship of Collingwood must be
listened to with caution and reserve, since he had the
character of being the best seaman in the fleet.*

Many illustrations might be given of the different
interpretations put upon the duty of service by Lord
Collingwood and Admiral Codrington. The latter
complains that the *éclat* of so grand a victory was
" frittered away," because the fleet was not sent home
immediately after the action was over: the "*éclat*" of
the victory being no doubt considered a very secondary
matter with Lord Collingwood, who had still hopes of
another engagement, and wished, if possible, to complete
the destruction of the combined fleets. Admiral Codrington says, " The disabled ships, which must of necessity go home, have a *kind of understanding* that they are
to go home by fives, without any ship to protect or assist
them if necessary ; and I must confess that I now envy
those who lost their masts in the gale after the action,

* Sir George Cockburn told Haydon the painter, that Collingwood was a better seaman than either Lord Nelson or Lord S.
Vincent. See ' Life of Haydon,' vol. iii. p. 237.

and who have come in here without having shifted
their sails, spliced their shrouds, or done anything to
make themselves efficient." "Had I lost my masts, as
the *Africa* did," he says in another place, "I should,
like her, have been ordered home."

He has another grievance also. He says that "being
asked by Admiral Collingwood what state we were in
the first time I saw him after the action, I answered
that we had knotted our rigging, fished our wounded
foremast, and helped ourselves out of the prizes to many
articles for which we were much distressed, and that
we were then fit and *ready* for any service whatever."
He then begins to complain to his friends that he was
detained on the service, confessing "it is a melancholy
thing to see so many other ships going home without
me," and mentioning another officer situated as he
was, "doing his utmost by all means in his power
to carry his point." Should we wonder that in such a
condition of things, Collingwood, being under the
necessity of maintaining the service as efficient as
possible, should take him at his word and retain him on
the station? About a year afterwards, during which time
he appears to have kept the sea, he had an interview
with Collingwood on the desirability of carrying his
ship to England; and, upon Collingwood disclaiming
knowledge of the bad state of his ship, Admiral Codrington said that he had not pressed it before, because
Collingwood had showed "a suspicion of his veracity."
However, he received a very polite letter from Lord
Collingwood the next morning, telling him to go to
England that evening. The way this was carried out
is singularly illustrative of the position of affairs.
Admiral Codrington says that "just at dark," when he

had finished sending away his stores, a nice breeze
enabled him to make all sail for the fleet. " Such was
my anxiety," he adds, " to be out of reach of his signals
on the next morning, that I *forced* the ship all night at
the rate of nine miles an hour against a very heavy
head sea, which made her labour more than she has
ever yet done since I have commanded her."

Animated by such a principle as this, it could, perhaps,
hardly be expected that one who went home to enter
into the gaieties and frivolities of London life could ap-
preciate the dignified and unostentatious reserve, the
uncompromising devotion to duty of a man like Collingwood, whose whole nature was bent in a totally
different direction; who, whilst the airy coteries of
London society were amusing themselves with the very
delirium and disease of pleasure, could watch through
long and weary nights on deck, or sit quietly and
painfully at his desk, and only think of home—of his
quiet home at Morpeth and his three dear ones there;
not forgetting, perhaps, old Scott the gardener and his
big cabbages.

If the reader will take the trouble to compare the
following letter, addressed by Admiral Codrington to his
wife in 1810, in its enumeration of the " *duties* " of a sea-
commander, with some of the letters given in this
volume, he will be able to observe still more clearly the
difference in character between Lord Collingwood and
Admiral Codrington. Perhaps he will also wonder as
much as I do, how the writer of it could say that Lord
Collingwood had " none of the *dignity* an admiral should
have," or what sort of significance he attached to the term.
The last clause of this remarkable code in particular
embodies an application of the principle of compensation,

which has at least the merit of newness and ingenuity.
The letter is as follows :—

"How curiously varied are the duties, obligatory and
voluntary, of a captain of a man-of-war! I am led to this
reflection by having, in addition to the constant minor
troubles of keeping together and victualling the ships under
my charge, just now had to read the burial service over a
man who died of a bowel complaint, and of my having, in half
an hour hence, to punish another man at the gangway; and
after praying in this solemn and expressive language, probably
before noon is announced some neglect in the work going on
may irritate me to swear like a trooper! I wish I could correct
myself of this blackguard practice; but I do really think it
impossible for any man to be alive to all the nicety of management requisite for this situation, without being subject to
irritation; and perhaps with such a despotic power as we
possess, it is as well for those subject to our lash that we
sometimes swear ourselves into the wrong, and by being
conscience-smitten, pass by without other punishment, as
venial, some of those errors which perpetually surround us.
However, I must say for myself that I never proceed greater
lengths for any mistake than damning a fellow for a fool, or
such like, and probably he suffers much less by the oath being
directed at him, than I do by the irritation it costs me in the
utterance."

Admiral Codrington, however, does ample justice to
Collingwood's gallantry. He says, after the battle of
Trafalgar, "Collingwood certainly went into action in
the finest style possible, and is as brave a man as ever
stepped on board a ship." He also says, "Lord Collingwood makes as great personal sacrifice to the service as
any of us; and I by no means assert there should be
any material sacrifice of the service to the comfort of
individuals." It seems a pity that this point of view

was not allowed its full weight generally with Admiral Codrington in judging the conduct and character of Lord Collingwood.

It may be added that no one, as far as I am aware, who knew Lord Collingwood intimately, has confirmed Admiral Codrington's view of his character; but quite the reverse. Abundant evidence that a very different opinion was unexceptionally held where he was really known by those fitted to form a true judgment of his character and abilities, has been given in this volume.

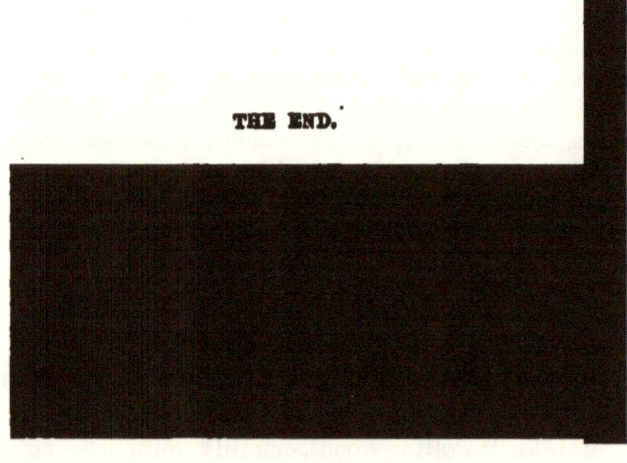

THE END.

LONDON: PRINTED BY WILLIAM CLOWES AND SONS, STAMFORD STREET
AND CHARING CROSS.

www.ingramcontent.com/pod-product-compliance
Lightning Source LLC
Chambersburg PA
CBHW060615030726
47498CB00005B/1689